Love Me Forever

A NOVEL

KASALAINI SAUVOU

authorHOUSE®

AuthorHouse™
1663 Liberty Drive
Bloomington, IN 47403
www.authorhouse.com
Phone: 1 (800) 839-8640

Published by AuthorHouse 12/17/2019

ISBN: 978-1-7283-3621-3 (sc)
ISBN: 978-1-7283-3620-6 (hc)
ISBN: 978-1-7283-3619-0 (e)

Library of Congress Control Number: 2019919598

Print information available on the last page.

CHAPTER 1

*H*E WAS A HANDSOME, VIGOROUS, AND YOUTHFUL LOOKING MAN. AND more than ever, he wanted to tell his parents about Delia. He had been teaching away from the mainland for three years, and it had served a useful purpose. It had given him all the time away that he needed; time he had used well to teach and to unexpectedly fall in love. He had been stalling his return to the United States for months and with Christmas setting in, he knew he couldn't delay much longer.

The time he spent teaching at the university had also served to remind him how passionately he loved teaching. Above all for Scott, the university and the students had provided both a means of escape and a gentle heaven. The beauty of this tourist island seemed to suit him far more than the festive or romantic night clubs back in the states which he had assiduously avoided.

His bags were packed in his car as he stood in front of the university, and familiar with the efficiency of the students by then, he knew that within hours of his departure, all evidence of his time abroad would have vanished. There were nine men and one woman in his class. He and the other university senior teacher had enjoyed a comfortable and respectful rapport.

"Sorry you have to leave now!" the other teacher said with a smile as he said goodbye to Scott.

He called Delia to say that he was on his way back to the apartment they shared in Savu. He often was distracted from the rigor of his studies by the image of Delia blowing through his mind like the island trade winds. His mind then was possessed with her simple beauty, the supple softness of her brown skin, the gentle way her hips swayed when she walked with him by the waves of the shore.

Scott got up very early the next morning and spoke with his parents in the United States about Delia.

"Of course, she is going to have culture shock. She's not going to like America at all because of the way she was brought up. It's not the racial barrier at all. When we get home, we'll talk about it".

His parents were worried. The next day he sat down with Delia and tried to explain to her everything. Delia assured him she wouldn't let it bother her.

"Everyone is entitled to his or her own opinion", she said. "In my country we don't have racial problems".

Delia and Scott began their long journey to the US mainland the next morning. He called his parents in Illinois to inform them that they were on their way to Chicago with a stopover in Hawaii. When the plane touched down at the Honolulu airport in

Hawaii, Scott and Delia took a cab to the Hawaiian hotel. It was one of Scott's favorite hotels.

Its ancient grandeur and exquisite service always reminded him somewhat of the Trigger Hotel back in the Savu Island.

He ordered room service shortly after they arrived. Torn between missing the comforts of the Savu Island and the excitement over meeting his parents in Chicago, they found it impossible to sleep that night. All they hoped for now was that his parents would accept and love Delia.

CHAPTER 2

*A*S SOON AS THE SUN ROSE OVER THE SPARKLING TURQUOISE OCEAN, they were up and dressed. They took a taxi from their hotel to the airport and Delia said nothing. Scott glanced at her.

"Why are you so silent?"

"I'm just contemplating about meeting your parents" she said. "I'm just worried that they won't accept me."

"Oh Delia, don't worry about my parents. The most important thing is that you and I are together" he said in a comforting voice while gently squeezing her hand. "I want you to relax and enjoy the flight. We have a lot to do when we get home".

The flight to Chicago took five hours and Delia slept most of the time while Scott read his Time magazine. The plane landed at O'Hare airport right on time, and Scott and Delia passed through customs quickly.

Despite Scott's long absence from the States, they had nothing to declare and looked tired as they picked up their suitcases. Delia stood next to Scott at the O'Hare airport in Chicago. It was six o'clock in the morning and nothing stirred. By eight the people would be moving in a vast space to catch their morning flights which would take them to their various destinations. Delia took a deep breath as she stepped onto the escalator leading down to the lobby where she was going to meet Scott's parents for the first time.

She loved this huge airport compared to the one back in Savu island. She had thought that first day she walked into the Christmas party, three years ago, that meeting Scott had been fortuitous. Quite by chance she had met the man of her dreams: handsome blue-eyed with a wicked grin. She paused for a moment. Delia glanced around the O'Hare airport, her hazzle eyes devouring everything-the different model cars, shapes, colors, people rushing in such beautiful and elegant attire. Within moments, Scott recognized the familiar form of his parents from out of the blur of travelers and eagerly introduced Delia.

"Delia! We are very delighted to meet you!" Scott's parents exclaimed. Delia grinned back at them.

"How was the flight?" Scott's father asked her.

"It was great! I slept most of the time" Delia told him.

They were all happy to see each other and specially to meet Delia for the very first time. "You are just in time for Christmas", Scott's mother told them as they climbed into their black Lexus SUV.

Scott conversed with his parents on the drive home, while Delia enjoyed the scenery with white snow on the trees and ground. The cold winter breeze brushed the light snow off the car windows as they drove on the freeway. Delia was hoping to plan a future with Scott and now she was struggling to adapt herself to her new life and family. They were very different from hers.

Scott revealed to his parents how he met Delia and how he had made up his mind to marry her. "But I haven't told Delia yet about my plans," he confided.

CHAPTER 3

*H*IS PARENTS WELCOMED DELIA, TREATED HER KINDLY AND WITH enormous understanding but as the days unfolded in their comfortable suburban home, things had been difficult for her: So many things to know, so many things to remember and a lot of things to learn. The most troubling "thing" of all was not knowing if Scott was ever going to marry her. Would his father Owen Riley and his mother Stephanie Riley accept her as a daughter-in- law? She was worried and continued to wrestle silently with these questions.

Delia knew that eventually she had to come to a decision. Her tourist visa was going to expire in the next six months, and she knew she had to share with Scott that she was experiencing a bad case of culture shock. Their lifestyle, the food they ate and the way they talked were very different from the way she was brought up. She wondered if she was going to adapt to their culture.

"I want to introduce Delia to Brian and Marian," Scott told his mother.

"No, I don't want you to do it yet", his mother warned him. "Delia is colored and these white folks will feel uncomfortable around her. You have been out of the country for a long time. You have to face the reality" she told Scott.

"I just don't think that they would have any problem with race. Delia is beautiful and people love to talk to her."

Just then Janet walked in, Scott's pretty sister with violet eyes.

"Hi Mom! Diane and I are taking Delia to dinner at a seafood restaurant near the lake", she said. "It's girls' night out-so sorry Scott!"

When the three arrived at the stately lakeside restaurant ironically named "The Seafood Shanty", Delia admired the beautiful decorations, especially the pretty white flowers in tall crystal vases on all the dining tables. The restaurant had wide glass windows in which she could see a very clear view of Lake Michigan.

After cocktails and a delicious dinner, Janet and Diane took Delia to an exotic night club where male dancers only performed.

"I haven't been to a male club before- this is my first time," Delia said. "You'll have fun," Diane told Delia.

As they arrived at the club, there were many women sittings down, waiting for the dancers to show up on the stage. They found an empty table at the front of the stage. Janet ordered Delia a drink called the "wall banger" and she bought herself a "screwdriver." Diane got herself a plain old whiskey and sour. It was a very cold winter night and it was snowing outside but the warmth of the fireplace and the energy coming from the dancers made this club the hottest spot in the city.

Five male dancers finally appeared on the stage and they were very good looking. The club was filled with laughter and music that was very sexual and romantic which could make anyone fall in love. The night was long as Delia watched the dancers move their muscular bodies towards them. The women were clapping their hands and laughing. Some of them gave money and tucked it into the men's bikini underwear, while others just threw five-dollar bills on the floor and watched in glee as the men bent over to pick up the tips.

The dancers had chiseled faces and beautiful muscular bodies. Delia felt cozy at the club. One of the dancers walked over and talked to Delia.

"You are very pretty. Where are you from?" he asked.

"I come from the Pacific Islands and I'm living with a friend here," she replied with a soft smile.

"Oh, that's why your hair smells like plumeria and jasmine!"

Leaning close to her delicately formed body, he sensuously whispered into her ear:

"My name is James Paul," he said as he purposely accented the "P" with a puff of warm air that ruffled Delia's hair and sent a shiver of excitement up her delicate neck.

He was very handsome with muscular shoulders, deep blue eyes and dark curly hair.

As he danced to another table of eagerly waiting women, he threw a brochure to Delia. "Here are my dance schedules - you can call me anytime".

"Wow! Jane exclaimed to Delia. "You are very lucky that he liked you! Most of the time, he doesn't want to talk to anyone."

The club was closing at one o'clock in the morning. Before they left the club, the dancer came back and flirted with Delia.

"Are you leaving?"

"Yes", replied Delia.

"I want to take you out for breakfast and then maybe back to my apartment."

"I am pretty tired but thanks for the invitation, maybe next time," she replied smiling. He walked them over to their car and said goodbye. Delia couldn't stop laughing.

"I don't know what I'm going to tell Scott about the evening. Maybe I will say it this way, "Scott, I met this crazy dancer who fell in love with me."

Janet and Diane both laughed at Delia. The three of them were pretty drunk. Diane was sitting in the back seat while Delia and Janet sat in the front seats. Delia had to get out first to let Diane out, but instead, she fell down on the snowy ground and could not get up.

Janet and Diane were laughing really hard.

"What's wrong Delia?"

"I can't get up!" "I'm stuck in the snow!"

Janet couldn't stop laughing at Delia! Both Diane and Janet went out and pulled Delia out from the snow. Delia could hardly move. They tried again and finally Delia got up and walked over to the car.

"Are you okay?" Janet asked Delia.

"I don't know, I must have drunk too much tonight and I have a horrible headache," she said with a slight slur in her speech.

As soon as they got home, Delia went straight to bed and didn't get up until late afternoon on the next day. Scott's dad told Janet never to take Delia back to the club because she had a bad hang over.

"You should have stayed home and helped my mother out," Scott said to Delia with a slight smirk.

"But Janet and Diane wanted to take me out and have a good time.

You know, life in this city is very different from my country. I really did have a very nice time last night," Delia told Scott.

"Great", said Scott reluctantly smiling.

Scott's family were wonderful people. They treated Delia very well.

CHAPTER 4

*I*T WAS TIME FOR SCOTT TO TAKE DELIA TO MEET SOME OF HIS BEST friends, Tim and Mary Jo. They were very happy to meet Delia. They all went to eat at the Light House restaurant where they served a variety of dishes: lobster, steak, fish, hamburger and chicken. The inside of the restaurant was very colorful with bright yellow walls and blue dining tables. They had beautiful green plants hanging down from the ceiling and antique chandeliers. After dinner, they took Delia to a Polish club and showed Delia how to polka dance. Delia really enjoyed it.

"You have to dance really fast when you do the polka," Scott told Delia as he whirled her around the dance floor, first dipping to the right and then dipping to the left, always counting *one* two three. Delia found this rhythm invigorating compared to the dreamy rhythms of her dances on the island. She also found the accordion to be a strange type of instrument. The musicians were pumping air in and out on what looked like a folded fan or a lung breathing while their fingers frantically pecked on keys like tiny birds eating scraps on the beach. The vigorous dancing made them all hungry for a midnight snack, so they grabbed a polish sausage with German mustard and washed it down with a pint of beer. They all went back to their friend's house, laughing and talking and drinking until four o'clock in the morning.

It was towards the end of April when Scott and Delia went to visit another old friend in Michigan. They left on a Friday afternoon and drove to Ann Arbor. Tom and Tatian were happy to see them. Tom had taken a sabbatical from teaching at the University of Michigan to teach astronomy at the Savu University. They all talked about the good old days they shared back in the islands.

"I will be going back to graduate school this fall at the University of Maryland," Scott announced. Both Tom and I are addicted to the college lifestyle. Delia and I are going to drive down to Maryland before school starts. We have to look for a place to stay as well. I have a friend who lives in Virginia and we'll probably go and stay with them until we find a place" Scott told his friends.

"That's great news," Tom said. "Stay in touch and let us know how things are going," he said.

Scott and Delia said goodbye to their friends and promised to stay in touch.

CHAPTER 5

SCOTT TOLD HIS PARENTS HE WAS GETTING READY TO GO BACK TO graduate school in Maryland. Scott confided to his mother what was on his heart.

"I'm worried about Delia. She looks unhappy and home sick. I am hoping she's going to like Maryland. We will have our own place then, so I think that might help her to feel more grounded."

"Let's hope for the best," his mother said.

Scott and Delia left his parents and began their journey to Maryland. Scott was doing all the driving. It took them one and half days to get to Scott's best friend's house in Virginia.

"We are very happy to see both of you! How do you like the United States so far Delia?" asked Cindy. Delia replied in a quiet voice: "I like it so far."

They stayed with Jack and Cindy for two weeks until they found their apartment in Maryland. The apartment was beautiful and conveniently located near the university bus line. Delia had never lived in an apartment all her life but she liked their new place. There were three other tenants living in the building.

Two weeks later, Scott started graduate school. They didn't have any transportation and it was hard on him. He had to take the shuttle bus every day. Delia was beginning to get bored. She learned the bus schedules right away and began to take the bus to go and see Scott at school and to shop at the mall. When Scott finally met some people at the university, they went out with them to dinner and bars, which was a welcomed change of scenery for both of them. He was still worried about Delia. She stayed home by herself and felt homesick most of the time.

Scott was relieved when they received an invitation from their neighbor downstairs to come and join them for their party.

The couple who lived below their apartment, Jackie and Tom, were both scientists and the man who lived across the hall, Marshall, was a biologist. Delia found them to be very strange, especially the biologist. Every day Scott went to school while Delia spent the day alone at home. As months went by, she was beginning to get really bored.

One day, she decided to take a walk to the nearest shopping center. It took her about thirty minutes to get there. She walked around the store and she finally saw two big grocery stores. One was called Giant food store and the second one was called Blueberry. She went first to the Giant food store and bought some fresh fish, fresh meat, potatoes and cabbage. As soon as she came out from the store, she heard someone saying. "Hi Delia!" She turned around and saw Marshall.

"What a nice surprise!" she called out. "What are you doing here?"

"I always come here to do my grocery shopping" he replied.

"Very nice store," she told him.

"Yes," he replied. "Can I give you a ride back home?"

"If you don't mind-"

"Not at all!"

"That's really nice of you," she replied.

"The next time you want to go to the grocery store, just let me know in advance, and I'll be more than happy to take you."

"Oh! Marshall-that's very nice of you," she said.

On the ride home, Marshall became strangely familiar with Delia-smiling, winking and asking many personal questions. "Where are you from Delia?" he asked.

"Savu Island - and that's where I met Scott."

"Why are you not married yet? You are a very attractive young lady!" Marshall told her in a way that made Delia feel uncomfortable.

"Thanks," she said with a slight blush caused by a mix of fear and vanity. He asked her about Scott.

"He is going back to graduate school," Delia told him.

"Oh! good for him. So, you will be alone most of the day," he said with a disturbing grin.

When they got back to the apartment, Marshall helped her inside with the groceries and she thanked him. She showed him back to the door as quickly as possible and as a precaution she mentioned that Scott would be home any second now.

Scott was always home around about five o'clock in the evening. Delia set the table and got everything ready for Scott. The doorbell rang and she quickly opened the door, and there was Scott. They hugged each other.

"I missed you very much," she told Scott.

"I missed you too, Delia," he replied kissing her and relishing the luminescent softness of her warm skin.

Scott was very happy about their dinner, especially the chocolate cake and ice cream for dessert. Scott asked Delia how she got the grocery shopping done. "I was getting bored sitting at home and I decided to walk down to the shopping center. I went over to the Giant food store and bought all the groceries there. As I was coming out the door, I met Marshall our neighbor. He then gave me a ride home.

"That was very nice of him", he replied.

"Yes, he was really quite helpful, in a strange sort of way."

Scott naively didn't recognize any threats to the safety of his beautiful vulnerable wife. He often looked at women abstractly like pleasures to be enjoyed in a man's free time. They watched the world news on the television before they went to bed.

CHAPTER 6

SCOTT USUALLY LEFT HOME AT EIGHT O'CLOCK IN THE MORNING IN ORDER to catch a ride with a fellow student. Everything seemed to be working out well for him. But by July, Delia's tourist visa was going to expire, and she would have to go back to the Savu Island. Every day, Scott thought about Delia's tourist visa, and how he could keep Delia in the States. Scott really loved her like a man loves a prized possession and he didn't want to lose her. He and Delia sat down one night and talked about it. "If you can't keep me here then I might as well go back home," she said. This thought made Scott realize what he must do. He called his parents and told them that he was going to marry Delia. His sister got on the phone and talked to her brother.

"I want you to make the right choice; we all liked Delia. She's a wonderful girl," she said to her brother.

But Scott wanted advice from his mother.

"Are you sure this is the right thing for you to do?"

"Yes, mother" Scott told his mother.

"I want you to think it over and let us know tomorrow what you and Delia have decided to do."

"Okay, mother, I will do that".

Scott and Delia couldn't go to sleep after he proposed marriage that night and Delia was very confused. All through Saturday while Scott studied in the den, she struggled with her conflicting thoughts: "My God! I'm too young to get married. I am not sure if I want to spend the rest of my life with Scott!" What happens if the marriage doesn't work out? What am I going to do?" Go back home and drive my parents crazy!" she started to cry. She called out to Scott to come to their bedroom.

"Scott, I don't think I can go through with this, just send me back home!" she cried.

Scott paused for a very long time.

"No, Delia, I don't want you to go back home. I'm in love with you! and I don't want anyone else! Please stay here with me! "I've brought you this far and we can't just give up on our relationship and our love," pleaded Scott. Delia finally calmed down and whispered softly as she collapsed into his arms.

"Okay, I will marry you."

Scott gently laid her limp body down on the bed, and enjoying this moment of sweet surrender, made love to her. When they had indulged their senses to completion, Scott wanted to further solidify their impending marriage. He rolled over, picked up the phone, and called his parents in Chicago to break the good news.

His father said that he was glad that Scott was finally measuring up as a man and taking responsibility for the island girl he brought to the states.

Scott's mother was very happy. She loved the idea of planning their wedding.

"We are going to prepare everything, and we are going to send the wedding invitations to all our friends and relatives" she told Scott and Delia.

CHAPTER 7

$\mathcal{S}$ COTT AND DELIA FLEW TO CHICAGO TWO DAYS BEFORE THE WEDDING. Scott's sister Jane came and picked them up from the airport. She was very happy to see them. Delia went and tried on her wedding dress. It was exactly made to fit her. The dress was a long lacey dress with short sleeves. The wedding was being held at Saint Mary's Catholic Church, near Lake Michigan. The white brick walls had blue stained-glass windows and the beautiful summer sunlight peering through would bring warmth to their wedding ceremony. On a hot August morning, all the one hundred guests began their journey to the church. The guests were led by the ushers to their designated seats. Scott's best men were Tom and Jerry, his friends from graduate school. Scott's father was standing next to them when he whispered in Scott's ear.

"Are you ready for this son?"

"Yes dad," replied Scott, taking a deep breath.

The pianist played *Shall We Gather at the River?*

Everyone stood up as the bride walked in.

Scott gasped in astonishment at Delia's radiant smile and graceful entrance. She looked beautiful. Her weddings dress showed her very slender body. Her maid of honor was her best friend, Dawn, and all the bride's maids wore pink dresses.

Delia's uncle flew from Savu Island to give her away and brought island flowers for the bride's headpiece and her bouquet: pink and white ginger and hibiscus and fragrant frangipani and plumeria woven about with bright green fern leaves. After the wedding ceremony, the couple stood in front of the church door while everyone walked by to wish them well on their way to the lavish reception at the Sheraton Hotel.

There was plenty of food to eat in the lavish buffet. Scott's mother had placed Savu Island dishes, like teriyaki chicken and grilled shrimp, around piles of fresh pineapple. The pineapple shells then became the holders for bouquets of yellow and pink frangipani and pink ginger flowers. She even hired an ice sculptor to carve a giant dolphin ice statue which she placed in the center of the buffet table and illuminated with colored lights. There were two crystal fountains pouring forth Mai Tai and Pina Colada cocktails. The band was playing classical and island music and everyone was enjoying themselves, dancing and laughing. Delia looked very happy and she wished her parents, who couldn't afford the travel costs, were there with them. She and Scott called her parents that night and told them all the details of the wedding and promised to send all the wedding pictures. They were very happy about the news and thanked Scott for marrying their daughter.

"I missed both of you and I wished you were both here," she tearfully told her parents.

CHAPTER 8

*T*HE COUPLE FLEW TO HAWAII FOR THEIR HONEYMOON. DELIA WAS VERY happy that everything about their wedding had turned out so well. They spent ten days in Hawaii drinking in the Aloha spirit and golden sunshine before they returned to Maryland. Three months later, Scott filed Delia's immigration papers so she could stay in the country. They went for an interview with an immigration officer and everything went well and within three months, Delia received her green card.

Delia found a county program right away where they trained people with different skills for six months. She saw a job opening with the County Housing Authority for a secretary in the engineering department. She called the personnel office and spoke with Patricia.

"I'm inquiring about the vacant secretarial job which was posted on the bulletin magazine yesterday," she stated trying to sound as experienced and professional as possible.

"We would like you to come for an interview and take a typing test tomorrow" said Patricia.

Delia was very excited and told Scott about the interview. Scott was very happy for her. Delia passed the keyboarding test and she did very well with her interview as well. "I will give you a call to inform you of our decision," Patricia said.

Delia went home and waited for the call. On the next day the phone rang and it was Patricia.

"Is this Delia?" she asked. "Yes! Delia answered in great anticipation.

"I am very happy to tell you that we are hiring you for the secretarial job, and we want you to start next Monday," she told Delia.

"I'm really looking forward to working for the county government," replied Delia.

She couldn't wait to tell Scott and she called him right away to break the good news. Scott was very excited and very happy for his wife. Delia was going to make thirty- five thousand dollars per year as a secretary for the manager of the engineering department. His name was Peter Fisher.

Scott invited two of his best friends from the university, Tom and Laura, to go out to dinner with them.

"I want to surprise my wife. She just got hired by the county housing authority to work for them," Scott told his friends.

They all went to Scott's house and found Delia at home.

"Surprise! We are taking you out to dinner!" they all shouted as they stormed in the door.

She was very excited. Scott made a reservation at the Windmill, a famous restaurant in downtown Washington D.C. They rode together in one car and got there about seven thirty in the evening. The place was packed with people. They had to wait for about forty minutes before they called their names out.

Everyone sat down at the table and enjoyed their food. Delia noticed the simple elegance of the restaurant with beautiful light pink water lilies placed on every table and all around. "They are the symbols of good fortune and prosperity," she thought to herself. After dinner, Scott invited Tom and Laura to spend the night at Scott and Delia's house.

The next morning, Scott told his friends, "I am going to serve you some New Guinea coffee which is the best in the world!"

"This really is a great coffee!" Laura commented. "It tastes mildly sweet and has that fruit aroma." After a delicious home cooked breakfast of turkey sausage and fried eggs, Tom and Laura went back to their home, while Scott and Delia went to the Smithsonian Museum in downtown Washington D.C. They had dinner at the Blackie restaurant before they returned home. Scott's mother already left them a message congratulating Delia on being hired for her new job. They both called her back, and she was really happy for Delia. They talked with Scott's mother for a while and she told them that they were coming down to visit. "Great, we are looking forward to seeing you!"

lia went to bed early on that Sunday night because she had to be in her new office at eight thirty in the morning. The alarm went off at six o'clock in the morning and Delia got up right away. She took her shower and got dressed. She wore a pink skirt, a white blouse and a pink jacket with a black pair of shoes. Scott was excited for her and told her for extra encouragement, "You look absolutely beautiful, Delia, so poised and professional!"

Delia laughed at his American "she's my trophy wife" attitude. He fixed them both a quick breakfast of scrambled eggs, a piece of toast and a cup of tea. Delia didn't have a very big appetite. Scott said she would be hungry later once her nerves settled down, so he fixed her a tuna sandwich for lunch. After breakfast, he got ready for school and drove Delia to work on that morning. When they arrived at her place of work, they embraced each other in a lingering hug. Delia said goodbye to her husband and told him that she would see him in the evening at home. Scott wished her good luck!

CHAPTER 9

ELIA ENTERED THE AUSTERE ENGINEERING OFFICE WITH SOME trepidation and introduced herself to the administrator at the personnel office. Marian took her around with the rest of the new employees and introduced them to all the departments. She took Delia to start working at her new office. Delia was met by Alice, who was about five foot tall and huge. Delia would be working with her. Alice gave Delia a quick tutorial and she began work right away. During the first week at her job, she met all her fellow workers. She met the two housing Inspectors, Brian and Rhonda. Rhonda was originally from India, and Delia and Rhonda instantly became friends.

The following week, she finally met her boss, Peter Fisher. He was tall and thin with a balding head and a pleasing smile. He stood very close to her, extended his hand and warmly welcomed her to their enterprise. Delia found him to be a very nice man.

Delia got paid twice a month. With her very first paycheck, she took her husband to dinner and afterwards to a movie. Scott was very proud of her. She started to save her money for a new car. She studied her driver's handbook and passed her driving test. Within three months, she bought a new Honda Accord with a light blue color. Delia registered herself at the community college to take a computer programming class. She was getting to be very busy during the day and the night as well. Within six months, she got promoted to the position of a data processing clerk, which really helped her financially.

Scott stayed busy at school and Delia stayed busy with her job and school as well. The only time she would see her husband was late at night but most of the time she would be in bed sleeping when Scott got home from school. Delia started to get new projects at work, and she began to get busier and busier every day. She made some new friends at work and hung out with them during lunch time.

She found out that most of these people had been working for the county for a long time. Alice, who was the head secretary at the Engineering department, found Delia one morning to inform her of the day's agenda. "I just want to let you know that Chris is looking for you."

"Who is Chris?" Delia asked.

"The new social worker!", Alice replied.

She gave Delia his phone number where she could reach him. She called him right away and spoke with him. He told her that he was wondering if she knew anything about a work order which he gave Matt, the maintenance man for the Orange Grove properties.

"He should have been out there yesterday to fix the tenant's window," she told him."

"I am going to check the window and I will call you back" he said to Delia.

He called back at three o'clock to let her know the work order had been done. Chris told her that he was coming to the office the next day and he would like to meet her. Delia told him she would be delighted. After she left from work, she went to the gym to do some exercise. She was beginning to stress out from her job.

She got home at five thirty in the evening and checked their messages on the phone. Scott had left her a message. "Delia go ahead and have your dinner. I'm going to be late tonight," he said. She didn't really like to eat alone. She cooked some fish, green beans and potatoes and went to bed early that night because she was tired. She had no idea when her husband was going to get home.

CHAPTER *10*

*D*ELIA SET HER ALARM CLOCK FOR SIX EVERY MORNING. SHE TOOK ONE more glance at her sleepy husband before she drove off to work. She was very busy that morning at work with many requests for maintenance repairs, like water leaks, broken windows, and fallen trees. Round about eleven thirty, just before their lunch break, Chris stopped by to see her.

He smiled at Delia. "You must be Delia!" he said. "I'm Chris Barron, the social worker for the county," he said.

"I'm very happy to meet you," she said.

He was about six feet tall and very well built. He mentioned to Delia about one particular tenant he was having a problem with because he just couldn't keep his house clean. He left trash everywhere and his lawn hadn't been mowed for months.

"What are we going to do with him?" Delia asked.

"We'll teach him cleanliness. He has been drinking too much thunder bird," complained Chris.

Delia laughed at him and he drew his body closer to her. Delia felt ashamed that she felt an immediate magnetic pull towards his warmth.

"One of these days you should come out and see our housing projects in the field," Chris told Delia.

"I'll be glad to," replied Delia gently smiling.

Then remembering that she was a married woman she said, "Well, I better get back to work."

Delia started to finish the work that was given to her that day. There were mostly work orders that had been completed by their maintenance workers, and she had to make sure that all the forms had been filled out properly before they sent the bills to the tenants.

She left work early on that day to go to school. She needed to study before her exams on the next day. Scott was home for a change, and she was very happy to see her husband. It had been two weeks since they had sat down together at the dinner table-let alone engaged in any intimate activity.

"Delia we are going out to dinner with bunch of people from the university tonight to the new Ethiopian restaurant. They all want to meet my wife! Delia laughed really loud.

"What's so funny about that?" Scott asked Delia.

"It sounds like the people I work with; they all want to see Delia!"

"Sweetheart you're young and very beautiful, and I know men will fall in love with you!"

"Scott, you are the only one I want to think I am beautiful and you need to be home more often to tell me. I want to go to bed now, Scott, I'm pretty tired. Can we make the dinner tomorrow evening?" Delia asked feeling despondent and starved, not for food, but for real intimacy with her husband.

The next day was Friday and Delia was looking forward to going out with Scott and his friends from school. Just at noon, Alice popped her head into Delia's workspace.

"Hey, Delia! Would you like to go to lunch at Hop Ty?" Alice asked Delia.

"Yes, I would love to," she replied.

Alice had worked at this place for ten years and she knew everyone.

My husband is a detective for the county, and we hardly see each other", she told Delia when their food arrived.

"I don't see my husband "the graduate student" very much either", Delia told Alice. They both grimaced and then offered sympathetic smiles to one another.

"I want to tell you something Delia!" Alice said, suddenly lowering her voice to make sure no one was listening to their conversation.

"Go ahead Alice!" Delia said emphatically. "Tell me your secret gossip."

"Well," she said slowly to draw out the suspense. "Well, I heard these guys were talking about you today," Alice told Delia.

"What guys?", Delia asked.

"None other than our big boss, Peter!"

"Oh dear, Alice. What did he say?" Delia asked fearing she had displeased her boss.

"I heard him telling Brian, the other Housing Inspector, how pretty you look,"

Delia breathed a sigh of relief and firmly said: "Well I hope everyone knows by now that I have a husband!" She was laughing in a sad sort of way. She emphatically added "and I love my husband very much, Alice!"

CHAPTER *11*

ELIA LEFT WORK AT FOUR O'CLOCK TO GO HOME AND BEGIN TO GET
ready for her dinner date. Scott got home around five thirty and
got himself ready as well. His friends came over at six thirty to pick them
up. There were about ten people all together. They were very happy to
meet Delia, Scott's wife. Their four cars headed to an Ethiopian restaurant
called Ababa.

The Ababa restaurant was situated in the center of Adams Morgan.
It was a very popular area for college students, visitors, and the locals.
The restaurant was huge and it could hold about two hundred and fifty
people. It was already packed with people before they arrived, but they
were very lucky to have already made their reservations. They waited for
five minutes before the restaurant hostess called them. They were led to
their table by a tall skinny Ethiopian waitress. She showed them to their
table and they all sat down and looked at their menu. They ordered honey
wine which is a traditional Ethiopian drink.

The menu was designed for clients to share different foods among
their friends or families. It was the traditional way Ethiopians would eat
their meals. They ordered stewed lamb, beef vegetables, and the house
special - spicy beef.

The waitress brought a big round dish and placed it on their table.

She brought their food selections with Ethiopian injera with typical
spongy texture. The waitress then put all the food on the injera in small
piles. They had to use their right hand only, small pieces of injera are torn
and used to grasp their stew and vegetables the same way the Ethiopians
would eat their food.

After dinner, everyone wanted to go dancing at this African night club called the Zebra, everyone except Scott that is. The club was owned by an African man who had created a multiracial club, but they mainly played different music from the continent of Africa. "Do you want to dance with one of my friends?" Scott asked Delia. "I would love to," replied Delia. "My wife loves to dance," he told his friends.

The club was right across from the restaurant and they didn't have to walk very far. As soon as they arrived at the door, the security guard asked for their ID. He let all of them in after paying the entrance fee of eighteen dollars. The club was huge and it had three different sections for dancing.

The first section played American music, the second section played African and Caribbean music, and the third section was a dining area with an adjacent dance floor. Delia loved the club and the different music they played. She danced with Tom, one of Scott's friends. People piled in at midnight. Delia liked the feeling of their bodies pressing together on the crowded dance floor. It made her forget that her husband was not dancing with her.

The club closed at two o'clock in the morning. Everyone left the club and headed for Jerry's Place to enjoy the best breakfast in town. Scott and Delia both ordered French toast, beef link sausage, coffee, and orange juice.

They all congratulated Delia once more for her new job before leaving, and she thanked them back. Delia and her husband arrived at their house at four am on Saturday morning. They slept until noon and did some cleaning around the house before Delia had to go back to school to do some studying while Scott stayed home.

When she got back home around six o'clock that evening, they had dinner and watched the world news on the television. The phone rang at eight o'clock and Scott picked up the phone; it was his mother. She spoke to both of them. His mother had to break the good news to Scott that his sister, Janet, would be getting married to Bob her fiancée that month. "I doubt both of us can make it to Chicago, but we will try to attend the wedding," Scott told his mother.

"If you want me to pay for your air fare, I will send you the money," Scott's mother told him with pleading disappointment in her voice.

"It's not the money mother- Delia and I have very busy schedules. She is working full time and going back to school at night now, and I am back at graduate school although my schedule is more flexible. We just don't see each other or spend time together anymore. I'm really worried that our marriage might not survive for the next six months! I think one of us can come, but it probably won't be both of us."

"Oh dear," Scott's mother opined. "Well, think about it and get back to us."

Scott hung up the phone and told Delia that he would like to go to his sister's wedding.

"How about you" he asked his wife.

"I don't think I will be able to go. I just have too many projects coming up at work and school too. Now that I am going back to school, I can't skip days," she told Scott.

"OK, I will call and tell my mother that you're not coming with me," Scott told Delia with a note of despondency in his deep voice and a sad look in his blue eyes.

CHAPTER *12*

*W*HILE SCOTT RETURNED HOME FOR HIS SISTER'S WEDDING, DELIA'S boss, Peter Fisher, asked her to accompany him to see some of the properties their company owned. "It is very important for you to see these properties. They will give you some idea what to say when the tenants call about the maintenance work, they need our department to fix for them," Peter explained to Delia.

She didn't have any idea what her boss Peter Fisher had in mind. Directly overhead, the sky was greyish blue but to the south, dark clouds were building. There was the danger of rain and strong winds blowing from the Chesapeake Bay.

"I estimate the storm will catch us within an hour'" he told Delia.

"I'm scared of storms!" she told Peter as he put his arm around her and pulled her closer to him on the front seat of his Mercedes.

"Don't worry Delia. I will take care of you," Peter said feeling protective of her fragility.

"What people don't realize, Delia thought to herself, is that I am really quiet an independent woman. It's just that I witnessed terrible storm tragedies on my island as a child and I'm needy because I am a foreigner in a strange country."

The storm finally arrived. Thunder rumbled as Peter directed them to a vacant house. They were not prepared for this storm. They had no umbrellas or raincoats to protect them from the rain. The dark sky was sparked with lightning flashes which looked like spider legs in the troubled sky. The storm was coming from the south. The rain at first was just a rhythmic splattering -but it quickly became an overpowering pounding. thunder, like a bass kettle drum, was booming in the background. The sound vibrations and cold water on her skin made Delia feel awake and strangely alive. The streets were flooded and water came from everywhere.

When they arrived at the house which he planned to show Delia, the water was rising very quickly in the nearby creek.

"Let's get in the house!" he told Delia.

They were both soaking wet when they got inside. The house was huge and had two fireplaces, five bedrooms, and four baths. The house had this strange smell of dampness because it had been vacant for so long. On the grass outside and in the tall pine trees, the winds of summer and storm continued to rumble. "I'm going to call the office. We are not going back because of the storm." he told Delia.

It was cold inside the house. Peter lit the fireplace and they both sat down to warm themselves. "Let's take our wet clothes off," Peter told Delia in a suggestive way. "There are some old towels and old sheets in this closet."

He grabbed a towel and threw it over to Delia. He spread the sheets near the fire place with two pillows. Delia dried her hair and her entire body.

"There isn't any place to hide except exposing ourselves to one another," Delia said.

Peter laughed at her. "I'm just not prepared for this," she told Peter. Delia stopped talking in her half naked awkwardness and finally Peter broke the throbbing silence.

"How come you're so quiet, Delia?" Peter asked in a seductive voice.

"I'm just thinking," Delia replied.

"About what?" Peter whispered as he inched closer.

"Us of course!" replied Delia.

Peter then told her, "You know, the very first time you walked into my office, I fell in love with you right away," Peter told Delia.

"Oh! really!" replied Delia. She didn't know how to answer him back. He was very direct and caught her by surprise.

"Yes, I wanted to take you out to lunch but I was too busy. I finally made up some ways to bring you out here," Peter told Delia.

Delia had been lonely for quite a while. Scott had spent too much time at school and he was always too tired when he returned home for any intimate time with her. Peter was very lonely with a sick bed-ridden wife at home and the only woman he wanted to turn to was Delia. Now Delia felt the "perfect storm" had arrived.

Conflicting emotions with conflicting desires came over her. She felt trapped. She felt that Peter had tricked her to come to this house so he could do anything to her. She wanted to distance herself as quickly as possible but he was her boss at work. Peter wanted to hold her and never let go. Delia was panicked. She was afraid.

"I don't want you!" she shouted. "I'm a married woman and I love my husband dearly!"

He stared at her while she fought back her tears. "I'm in love with you Delia!" he said.

"No" she said, as she turned away.

"Peter, how can you say you love me when you have only known me for thirty days?"

But Peter put his arm round her drawing her back against him. Peter reached over and kissed her passionately. He pulled her on top of him and slipped inside her. She grinned. They moved together. "This feels really good," Peter said. It's a shame to stop now when we just learning about each other."

"Oh! don't worry," she said breathlessly as her hips began moving faster, "by the time we're done, we will know all there is to know about each other." He rolled over on top of her without losing his place. "I think you're the skinniest woman I've ever made love to," Peter said. "Do you like me?" she asked. "There isn't anything I don't like about you. You are unique and beautiful" he said. Peter was sensing that she was about to come and moving faster. Delia began to cry out his name like a Hindu Mantra and in a moment they came together.

CHAPTER *13*

*T*HE STORM FINALLY STOPPED AND THEY HAD TO RETURN TO THEIR families. They said goodbye and went on their separate ways. Delia got home and there was no Scott. She went and filled up the bathtub with warm water and she soaked her tired body. She kept thinking with guilty pleasure about what she had done with Peter. The phone rang. She rushed to grab it, thinking it might be her husband. But it was Peter.

"I wanted to know if you are alright?"

"Yes, I'm okay, and thank you for calling me," she told Peter. She went to bed early that night.

When she arose at six o'clock the next morning, she looked at her tired husband lying next to her. She touched his face, kissed his forehead and left for work.

Peter stopped by her office to see her. "Would you like to go out for lunch?" he asked. "Maybe next time," she curtly replied.

Delia had decided to go back to college to finish her computer science degree. She had only one semester to go before she received her diploma. She had made up her mind that morning to leave no room for Peter to ask her out. She went and registered at college and started going back to school the following week. She met many old friends at school and they were glad to see her again. She was determined to finish her computer science degree.

She thought about how her husband Scott and her boss Peter were so different from each other. Peter was in love with her and wanted to spend more time with her, but Scott her husband seemed to be tied up at school all the time and didn't have time for her. She was afraid that Scott was drifting away from her. Their marriage was sifting like sand through her fingers. She had to face Peter every day at work. Her fixation on Peter simply wasn't healthy.

Scott was not there for her and the only man who seemed to care about her was Peter. She straightened out her back, focusing on her work to get through the day. Peter called her into his office. Delia got up and walked into his office. She knew Peter was going to ask her out again. "Please sit down," he said tenderly. "Delia, I know you don't want to see me and I know you've been avoiding me the last two weeks" he said.

"That is not true," Delia protested. "I am going back to school to finish my computer science degree. I want a better job."

"I love you Delia and I want to be with you. I want to spend more time with you."

"I have to make some hard decisions next week about my marriage," she said. "I feel my husband Scott is drifting away from me. I know he is very busy at school as well. I feel that he is putting school before our marriage. But I'd rather have you stay away from me. I need to be alone to process all my feelings and plans. I don't want to see you anymore. Can't you understand that I need to sort my life out?"

Peter stared at her while she fought back tears. "I love you Delia!" he said so quietly it could barely be heard.

Tears spilled out and rolled down Delia's cheeks. "No!" she said turning away from him.

Peter held his arm around her. "There has never been anyone for me but you. It kills me when you ignore me, Delia. I need you in my life," he said.

"I need to be alone," she said.

"We belong together" he murmured burying his face in her hair.

"You're wrong," she said flatly while pushing him away. "Has it ever occurred to you that I have a husband whom I love very much," she said. "That affair was a mistake and I don't want you to touch me anymore."

Ripping himself away from her, Peter headed for the door. "I won't beg anymore," he said in a proud but wounded voice.

Delia slumped down on the couch curling on her side; she buried her face in a pillow and wept. Peter returned to his work supervision as stoically as possible, but inside he ached for Delia-for her body and her soul.

CHAPTER 14

ELIA TRIED TO STAY BUSY WITH HER SCHOOL WORK FOR THE NEXT month but the thoughts about her dying marriage occupied her mind one evening. She couldn't concentrate on her studies. She looked at the clock and she thought it was not too late to call Peter. The phone rang for a while before Peter picked it up. "Are you still awake?" she asked.

Oh my God, Delia," he said. "I was not expecting to hear from you after that fight we had last month," he said. "I'm sorry that I behaved the way I did."

"I just have been going through so many different things. You know, my marriage and school," she said. "I'm hoping that you understand."

"Delia, my love for you hasn't changed; I'm still in love with you," he told her.

"Would you come and meet me at the Green Bar for a drink?" she asked.

"Sure, I will be right there!"

Delia was delighted. She couldn't hold herself back anymore - she had to share her lonely heart with Peter.

He was punctual. She met him at the door. They both sat down at the table near the window facing the Atlantic Ocean.

"What would you like to drink?"

"A whisky on the rock," she said.

The waiter brought their drinks over and set them on their table. Delia admired the ocean waves and the beautiful full moon shining over the Atlantic Ocean. "I'm very happy that we are together again Delia," Peter said, as he put his arm low on her waist in a very familiar way.

"We're not exactly together, but at least we are not fighting!" Delia quipped.

"It looks like you have a lot on your mind, Delia," Peter said with genuine concern.

"Yes, I have a lot to tell you tonight," she replied "I can't hold it anymore but I need to share it with you," she told him.

"My marriage is in limbo right now. We don't sit down and talk. We don't see each other. Scott spends a lot of time at school now with different projects. He doesn't call me anymore to let me know what is going on with him. We are just two strangers living together. I'm going to file for divorce," she told Peter.

"Delia, you can't just go and file for divorce, you should have a strong ground and reason for divorcing your husband."

"I have good reasons," she replied.

"You better find a very good lawyer to help you," he said.

"What if Scott has found out about my affair with you Peter? Knowing him, he wouldn't want to hurt me but he definitely would feel angry and betrayed."

"What are you going to do then?" Peter asked Delia

"Nothing," she said. "But the best thing for you to do is to stay away from me" she told Peter.

"Why?" he asked Delia.

"Because this love affair we're having is not going anywhere. Besides if people found out about us at work, it could cause problems You know, I love my husband very much and I just won't give him up for anything or for anybody!" Delia cried. "I know you are feeling the same thing about your wife. She has been sick for a very long time, and there's no way you are going to walk away from her. Our love affair is a dead-end street! I'm going back home now," she told Peter.

She left him all alone at the Green Bar. Peter sat silently and strange thoughts started creeping in his mind. "My God, I'm really in love with this woman. I have never felt this way with anyone else before. Maybe it is only because she is young and beautiful," he thought to himself. He left a five-dollar tip for the waitress and walked back to his car in the shadows of the night.

CHAPTER 15

ELIA WAS NOT FEELING WELL THE NEXT AFTERNOON, SO SHE LEFT THE office early and went home. She took some aspirins and went to sleep. Scott arrived home early and found her sleeping soundly. He did the laundry and cooked some fish for dinner. Delia got up at six in the evening and she was very surprised to see her husband at home so early. She began to get panicked. Strange thoughts beginning to creep into her mind. "What am I going to do? Scott probably knows about my affair with Peter. Oh no! this is horrible! What am I going to do? How am I going to tell him the truth?"

She started crying and went to the bathroom and she got sick to her stomach. She felt queasy and dizzy like she was having an anxiety attack, but she knew the terrible truth- the chemical abortion pills had begun to work. She heard Scott calling her.

"Delia are you alright? Your dinner is ready."

"I'll be right there," she said.

She changed her clothes and went to see her husband in the kitchen.

"Well, this is a nice surprise that we are both home early and my husband is cooking dinner for me," Delia told Scott.

"Yes, it is really a nice surprise," replied Scott giving her a cursory hug and peck on her cheek.

"What's wrong with you Delia?" asked her husband.

"I just felt really sick at the office and came home early. I took some aspirins and went to sleep," she told Scott.

He was silent and he kept looking at her in a very strange way which made Delia very uncomfortable. She kept on watching the world news on the television. Scott asked if she was going to work in the morning. She told him that she was.

They both went to bed and Scott slept like a rock but she couldn't go to sleep at all. She felt guilty for what she had done and started crying. Delia got up very early the next morning and left for work while Scott was still sleeping. She couldn't concentrate on her work. She was thinking about her husband and wondering if he already knew about her affair with Peter.

CHAPTER 16

SCOTT JUST COULDN'T BELIEVE WHAT THE NURSE HAD TOLD HIM. HE felt like someone stabbed him in the stomach. "I should blame myself for this. If I only had tried to come home early and spend more time with Delia, if I only had told her that I loved her very much- If I had only made more time for love making, maybe this wanton affair with her boss would never have happened.

I have been very selfish towards my wife," he cried out loud and felt sorry for himself. He wanted to go and confront Peter Fisher, Delia's boss, for making his wife pregnant. He wanted to report it to the local newspaper to embarrass the county executives that some of their married workers needed to be investigated for cheating on other employee's wives, but he changed his mind.

"Thank you very much for your help," Scott told the nurse.

When he returned home, he thought about taking a trip abroad to escape the nightmare. Scott looked for his passport but he couldn't find it. He wanted to call his wife- maybe she put it somewhere else but he was too upset to call her. He decided to ask her when she came home from work. Scott went to school that afternoon and returned home early. Delia came home about six o'clock with a terrible headache. Scott was already home when she arrived. He asked right away about his passport. She told him that she put it in the last drawer. He then told her that he went through every drawer but he couldn't find it. She was panicked. "You did what Scott?"

"I went through every drawer and as matter of fact, I took everything out."

"What do you mean you took everything out?" she asked.

"Yes, I took everything out including your pills." Delia was silent.

"How long were you hiding something that you didn't want me to see?" Scott angrily asked. Delia was very silent. A very unpleasant and cold atmosphere entered their room at that moment filled with blame and guilt -woundedness and anger. Delia shivered and trembled uncontrollably. How could he ever trust her again? She began to cramp and became crippled with pain-physical and emotional. She dragged herself to bed realizing that Scott had shut down and would not come to comfort her.

The next three months they didn't have any sex. Scott was basically very busy at school and Delia was also very busy with her job. Each day, they both were drifting farther apart. Each day, Delia started to get lonelier and every day she was getting closer and closer to Peter Fisher. She was beginning to spend more intimate time with Peter her boss than with Scott her husband.

Delia began to think she was in love with Peter. She spent every day of the week at work with him, while Scott spent more time at school every day. Delia was glad she had decided to go back to school to finish her computer science degree class. She had only one semester left before she could graduate and become more independent.

CHAPTER 17

NE EVENING WHEN DELIA RETURNED FROM HER COMPUTER CLASS, HER girlfriend Victoria called. She asked Delia if she felt like going shopping in downtown Washington D.C. the next Saturday. Delia told her yes but she asked her to come and pick her up from her house. Delia was looking forward to seeing Victoria. They had met in her hot yoga class and although they were opposites in many ways, they quickly became close friends. Delia appreciated the sage advice Victoria could offer from her grounded perspective. Delia always seemed to be floating or fleeing like a free spirit in search of artistic expression. Sometimes Delia felt she was cursed with beauty and emotion while Victoria was blessed with brains and common sense.

Victoria arrived at ten o'clock on Saturday morning to pick her up.

"Delia you look very pale, what's the matter? Victoria asked.

"I have been very sick lately," she replied.

"Have you been to the doctor?".

"No, not recently," Delia replied, feeling guilty that she couldn't share the truth with her friend. "I'll be OK. I just need to rest. I have been under a lot of strain lately.

Hoping to shift the spotlight, Delia asked "How is your work going Victoria?"

"Great," Victoria replied. "I love being an attorney who can help people solve their legal problems."

"How is your married life?" Victoria asked with the directness of an attorney cross examining a witness.

"I just don't know anymore, Vic," Delia replied truthfully.

"Why? What's the matter?"

"I just don't know if Scott and I will be able to save our marriage," Delia said.

"Why, What's the matter?" Victoria asked again.

"I'm very confused, Vic."

"About what?" asked Victoria.

"It's a very long story and I can't tell you right now. I will tell you when everything is calmed down. But in the meanwhile, I have decided to go back to school and finish my computer degree class. I only have one semester left. I am going to be taking meditation as well. I really need these extra activities to help me stay focused and strong as well.

"I am glad that you are establishing healthy goals, Delia!".

They had lunch at the Cafe Royal, one of the most popular restaurants downtown. After they finished their lunch, Delia told Victoria that she wanted to go home because she was feeling unwell. Victoria drove them back to the house and she visited for a while. Victoria was just gathering her belongings to leave when Scott showed up. He was happy to see Victoria.

Delia was lying down in their bedroom. Victoria told Scott that Delia hadn't been feeling great the whole day. "When we went shopping downtown, she began to feel bad. She then asked me to bring her back home and said that she needed to rest."

Delia rose up when she heard Scott's voice. She got out of bed and came to the living room. She was very happy to see her husband home on a Saturday. Scott asked her if she was feeling better. She told him that she was now that he was home.

Scott went to get some Chinese food for dinner while Delia and Victoria set the table and made some tea as well. Scott returned home with the food within thirty minutes. They all sat down and ate. Delia finally felt hungry and she finished all her food. They had ice cream and cake for dessert.

After Victoria helped Delia clean the dishes, she was ready to go home. Before she left, she asked Delia if she wanted to go the farmer's market the next day. "Okay", replied Delia. "I'll come and pick you up in the morning," said Victoria.

CHAPTER 18

ELIA WENT TO BED EARLY THAT NIGHT BECAUSE SHE WAS FEELING terrible again. She took some aspirins and went to sleep. Scott stayed up for a while watching the television. They both got up very early on Sunday morning. Scott fixed their breakfast that morning. He told Delia that he had to go to the university to do some work and he should be back home round about six o'clock in the evening. Victoria came by to pick up Delia around nine o'clock in the morning.

The farmer's market was held in Rockville. There were so many people at the market. The two best friends bought fruits and vegetables, and then they went and had some fish and chips at the nearby restaurant. Victoria asked Delia again.

"What's really wrong with you Delia?"

"I just can't tell you right now, Vic; it's just too complicated and sad to tell you at this time. Besides, I am just not in the mood to tell you. It's too sad and scary."

"It must be really bad," Victoria commented.

"Yep", it is," Delia nodded in agreement. "These fish and chips are really tasty, Vic. We should come here more often. I'm going to be on vacation within the next two weeks," Delia said, successfully changing the topic of discussion.

"Do you have plans to go anywhere?" Victoria asked Delia.

"Yes, I will probably go to New York and visit some friends, and I want to go to Europe," said Delia.

"Where about in Europe?"

"Italy, France and England. I've always wanted to visit these countries."

"Let me know when you go, maybe I'll travel with you," said Victoria. "How about Scott, is he going with you?"

"I doubt it very much- he has too many things to do at school," replied Delia sadly.

Victoria took Delia home and went back to her place. Delia was feeling bad again. She was having very bad cramps and a terrible head ache. She took some aspirin and went to sleep. She got up late Monday morning and arrived at her office at nine o'clock.

As soon as she got back to the office, Peter called her on the intercom to come and see him right away. She went to see him as soon as it was possible.

"I have something to tell you. I put in my resignation today," he announced to Delia.

"You what! Oh really?" Delia was shocked and surprised. "How come?" she asked in disbelief.

"I really have this strange feeling that they are going to fire me," Peter confessed.

"Did you talk to anyone about it?" Delia asked.

"I talked with someone today and he told me that they were going to let me go soon," Peter told Delia.

"Well, think of it in a positive way. Maybe it's the best thing for you," she said to him.

"You are probably right," said Peter.

"Have you got something lined up already?" she asked.

"No, not really. I have decided to go home and take it easy for a while. Sandy, my wife hasn't been feeling well lately. I want to be home with her for a while before I go back to work," said Peter to Delia.

"Good for you! - that's really nice for you to do something good for your wife. You haven't been really spending too much time with her," said Delia.

Delia went back to her desk and was happy that Peter was resigning. She had this feeling, if he didn't do it, their love affair was going to be exposed very soon. There were too many people who were suspicious and were watching them like a hawk.

CHAPTER *19*

O N THE NEXT MORNING, DELIA RECEIVED A MEMORANDUM ABOUT PETER'S going away party. Their department was taking him out to lunch the next Tuesday. They already made the reservation at this seafood buffet called "Ocean Blue" on East West Highway in Bethesda.

Peter's last day would be next Friday. Delia tried to finish all her work before she went on vacation at the same time as Peter's last week at work. "I don't really care what people are going to say," Delia muttered. "I already planned my vacation before he decided to leave," she said defiantly to herself.

The goodbye lunch was great! And everyone wished Peter well. People gave him all kinds of gifts like flowers, plants, and books.

The engineering department president, Donald Rice, gave a very long speech and thanked Peter for the wonderful job that he had done for the county. There were three other speeches and then everyone left to go back to the office. On this last day, Delia went to say goodbye to him at his office. They both got very emotional with each other and promised to stay in touch. They knew they wouldn't be conveniently seeing each other every day at work anymore. It was just so painful for Peter to leave Delia. She didn't know what to tell him. He made her pregnant which caused her to have a painful abortion but deep down inside her, she still cared for him. She let him go and went home crying. As soon as she got home, she saw a message from her husband. He had gone to Baltimore and would be calling her from there that evening. She took her shower and went to sleep. The phone had been ringing for a while before she picked it up and it was Scott.

"Something is wrong with the car," he told her.

"What is wrong with the car, Scott?" she asked.

"The engine light is on and I don't think I'm able to come home tonight. I'm going to take it to the car repair here in the morning. "I'll see you tomorrow," he said.

Delia looked at the clock. It was ten o'clock at night. She fluffed her pillow and rolled over in their half empty bed, feeling restless and vaguely agitated. The phone rang again and she quickly picked up the phone and it was Peter. She was happy to hear his voice.

"What are you doing?" he asked. "I'm in bed and ready to go to sleep," she said dreamily. "I was talking to my husband just before you called. He's spending the night in Baltimore. The engine light of the car is on," she said.

"Really! "So, you are alone? Peter asked Delia eagerly.

"Yes," she replied.

"Why don't you come and meet me? I will turn my engine light on for you," he said half teasing her.

"Where about?" she asked turning over in her bed.

"In Silver Springs," said Peter.

"That's not very far from here. Will you come and pick me up. I'm not in a good mood right now."

"Okay, I'll be there in twenty minutes,"

Delia was happy to see Peter. They went to the River City bar. They both expressed how they missed seeing each other. They continued their conversation from where they left off during the day.

"I love you very much and I think about you every day. I have been thinking about divorcing my wife" Peter told Delia.

"It wouldn't be fair to do that to her. She is sick!" Delia told Peter.

"We just can't have each other in a permanent way," she told Peter.

"I can't leave Scott right now!" We would have so much to lose" she told him.

"Do you think he's seeing someone else?" Peter asked, hoping to burst her bubble of denial.

"Sometimes I feel he is. He hasn't made love to me for about four months now," she said.

"Do you think he knows about us?' Peter asked.

"Yes, he knows that I made a terrible mistake with you and that I tried to hide my mistake by having an abortion. He was very angry at you at first and then he just shut down towards me. And now he makes himself very busy with university projects," Delia said. "We had dinner with his friends last month and his friend asked him about going to Baltimore for some extended workshop," she explained.

"When are they going to start the workshop? asked Peter.

"I assume very soon. I just can't see our marriage lasting more than a year from now," Delia confided to Peter.

"Delia, I really need to stay in touch with you because I truly love you. You know I will never give up hoping that we will be together some day," Peter said.

She was silent for a very long time. "Probably the best thing for us to do is to go our separate ways. After what I went through with you, the pregnancy-the horrible painful abortion, I just don't feel it is right for us to see each anymore," Delia said.

"Delia, you are out of your mind. Do you think that I'm just going to forget you just like that! I love you very much Delia, you are the best thing that has ever happened in my life. I want to see you all the time, and please, don't stop me!" Peter cried out.

"I don't know if I am the best thing to happen in your life but I do think I am the most convenient thing to happen in your lifeless marriage. Okay, let's leave this conversation there -I have to go home now. I am just not feeling good right now," said Delia.

CHAPTER 20

*P*ETER TOOK HER HOME AND TOLD HER THAT HE WAS GOING TO CALL IN the morning. They said goodbye, and Delia went straight to bed. She felt tired and sick.

She took some aspirins and went to sleep. She heard the phone ring and it was her girlfriend, Victoria.

"Are you in bed?" she asked.

"Yes, I am. What's up?" she asked.

"Can I come over?" Victoria asked.

"Sure, Scott is not here- he went to Baltimore, and he called to tell me that something was wrong with his car. He is spending the night over there," Delia complained.

"That's a brand-new car! What was wrong with the car?" Victoria skeptically asked.

"The engine light was on," replied Delia.

"Oh, that's a good story. I think your husband is having an affair with someone."

"Are you sure about that?" asked Delia.

"Well I would call it circumstantial evidence. Look at it this way, he didn't tell you the engine light came on until ten at night and that's a brand- new car. He has only been driving it for two months now," Victoria reasoned.

"I am trying to be very positive about this, Vic. You know, new cars too can have problems."

"Maybe you are right, Delia! Maybe I am just jumping to conclusions, but I doubt it."

Scott arrived at noon. He looked very tired. Delia was already at work. Scott took his shower. After he dressed, he left for school. He called his wife. "I'm going to Baltimore tomorrow morning for our workshop. I will be down there for the whole week," he told Delia. She was quiet for a very long time and finally spoke up slowly.

"Where will you be staying?" she asked.'

"'I will be staying at a hotel with the rest of the people from school."

"How long is the workshop?" she asked.

"About a month, but I will try to come home on weekends," he said without emotion.

"We need to talk Scott."

"Delia, I know. I have been too busy doing my schoolwork and I don't spend enough time with you," he replied robotically.

"I'm really worried about our relationship and I've noticed you've changed so much and I'm worried about our marriage," she explained.

"We'll talk when I get home," he told Delia in a slightly impatient tone of voice. Delia thought for moment she heard a girl's voice whisper in the muffled background noise on the phone.

CHAPTER *21*

$\mathcal{S}$HE GOT UP VERY EARLY IN THE MORNING AND CALLED VICTORIA. "LET'S meet at the Rainbow Cafe on East West Highway at eight o'clock."

It had been raining hard outside and there was a thunder storm brewing. She was thinking about Scott while she drove. The salty tears in her eyes blurred her vision as she tried to think about their marriage slipping away like sinking sand. Victoria was already waiting for her at the cafe.

They sat down and ordered their breakfast right away.

"Are you alright, Delia?" asked Victoria.

"Yes", she replied weakly.

Victoria then asked about her husband.

"He will be in Baltimore all this month for their workshop," Delia said.

"Really!" Victoria said incredulously.

"But he said he would try to make it home for the weekend."

"Do you really believe him Delia?'

"I don't know what to believe anymore," she said. "Victoria, will you come and stay with me until he comes back at the end of the week.?"

"I will, Delia, because that's what best friends do for one another."

Delia was glad that Victoria would be staying with her. She had a secret to share with her. She felt it was the right time to tell her very dear friend.

When they had returned to the privacy of Delia's apartment and made a pot of tea, Delia confessed: "Victoria, I have a secret that I want to share with you. I have been keeping this secret to myself. It is just a horrible, sickening, betraying and stupid secret," Delia told Victoria.

"I just can't believe you're sounding like this," she said.

"Vic, sometimes we wonder how we do stupid things in our lives. Are you ready to hear my story?"

"Sure," replied Victoria.

"You see, Vic, for the last nine months, I have been having an affair with my boss at work. It got so bad that he made me pregnant and I have had a horrible abortion with pills. I just can't believe that I had let myself go that far. He is a married man and his wife is very sick at home. He can't make love to her anymore. I was lonely too with my husband staying out for long hours at school. I was always alone at home. I was lonely and he was the only man that I was very close with at work.

Delia started crying. "I love my husband dearly; I just don't know where our marriage went wrong. He found out about my pregnancy -but he hasn't confronted me about it yet."

"How did he know about it?" Victoria asked.

"Vic, you know, Scott is very intelligent. He was looking for his passport one day, and he took everything out from our dresser drawers which included my stuff as well. We both share the same dresser drawers.

He found everything about the abortion clinic and my pills. He called the clinic and they told him everything," said Delia

"How did you know about it?" asked Victoria. "the nurse from the clinic called me and told me everything," said Delia.

"Oh my God, Delia! that is horrendous and he hasn't asked you or mentioned anything about it?" asked Victoria.

"No, but knowing, Scott, he will ask me anytime now because I know he's up to something now. I just know it by the way he has been behaving lately and especially this morning. I feel tortured by my foolish deeds. I told Peter that I didn't want to see him anymore," Delia told Victoria.

"Wow! No wonder you felt bad all last week. I was wondering why you were getting sick all the time,"

"I am still recuperating from this horrible procedure and complications. I'm afraid that Scott is going to leave me and I don't want to be alone and I don't want to start my life all over again. It's going to be really hard on me," Delia told Victoria.

"Look at it in a very positive way. You have a very good job, and you can get on with your life. You will meet someone better than Scott," said Victoria.

"I don't think I'll ever want to get married again," said Delia. "I will probably move to a different state."

The next morning, after they finished breakfast, Victoria asked Delia if she wanted to go with her to New York on the weekend. Delia agreed. Victoria went back to work, and Delia went downtown to escape from her depressing reality. She did some mindless shopping at the mall and went back home. Scott had returned from the workshop for a day

But he left her a note stating that he was coming home late because they had an open house for the astronomy department. She took a long nap that afternoon.

The phone rang and it was Peter. He was calling to see if she was all right. "Everything is fine," she said.

"I miss you," he told her. "I hope you change your mind, Delia. about being with me," he said.

"Peter, I don't think we should see each other anymore and I feel my marriage is over. I don't want to do anything with you anymore! Look at all the problems you've caused me and you didn't even do anything to help me."

"Delia!" He yelled. "I've told you so many times that I would marry you whenever you are ready," Peter said.

"How could you marry me, when you couldn't even divorce your wife? And you know, there is no way in the world you would do that!

"Delia just tell me what you want, and I will do it," he said.

"No, Peter you have to make your own decisions. The best thing for you is to forget me and let me go on with my own life. I love my husband, and there is no way in the world that I could just walk away from him. I have this strong feeling that Scott is ready to tell me something which I am not going to like at all. His brother is coming in August. He hasn't really told me why his brother is coming to see us and I haven't really asked him. Scott's brother, Steve, talked to him two days ago and he didn't even say anything to me. I was very suspicious about that. Scott must have told him and probably his parents as well. Do you see what you have put me through?" Delia said.

"Delia! Get rid of him!!" Peter shouted.

"It's very easy for you to say," said Delia. "Scott and I had been together for three years before we got married and I find it very hard to just let him go. I want him to tell me the truth- that it was my fault," Delia cried out with tears welling in her beautiful vulnerable eyes.

"Okay, Delia, do what is right for you and I wish you good luck!" They said goodbye and as soon as she hung up the phone, she screamed into the empty air:

"Oh my God what have I done, what have I done dear God! I didn't want this to happen to me! Why? Why did I let these things happen? I care about Peter very much but he's a married man. I love my husband, Scott, and I don't want to lose him," Delia cried.

"Please dear God, you have to help me, and I ask for your forgiveness."

CHAPTER 22

*A*T THE END OF THE WEEK, ON THE OTHER SIDE OF TOWN, PETER WAS at the Western Grill Bar on Wisconsin avenue with a glass of beer in front of him. He was thinking of Delia as he watched the people dance on the large wooden floor. The juke box was playing the Rolling Stone song, "This will be the last time, may be the last time, I don't know." He felt Delia's presence around him; he felt very lonely with tears welling in his eyes. He wanted to call her but he just didn't have the courage to do it.

He sat around for a while crying into his beer, hoping to drown his sorrow in alcohol, looking down on an empty barstool next to him, tortured by the sound of other couples laughing and dancing. When he finally looked up, he saw two women walk in the door. He jumped out from his seat -one of them really looked familiar to him.

"Oh my God! That's Delia!" He was right. It was Delia and Victoria.

They didn't see him because the house was packed with people. It was eleven o'clock on Friday night. This bar was one of the most popular and upscale hang outs for everyone in the city, young and old.

The female friends found a table near the corner across from him. Peter noticed that Delia was drinking ginger ale. They were looking at the people on the dance floor. Peter couldn't help it anymore. He stood up and went to see them.

"Peter," yelled Delia. "What are you doing in here?"

"What are you doing here yourself?" he asked, raising his voice to be heard above the loud music.

"I want you to meet my girlfriend Victoria."

He was happy to see Delia as if a silent prayer had been answered.

"How long have you been here?" she asked.

"Right after I talked to you over the phone" he said to Delia.

"Peter, you have been here almost all night!"

They didn't say very much to one another because of Victoria. He asked Delia if Victoria knew about their illicit relationship.

"Yes, but I don't think she knows that you are my boss at work who I have been having this affair with," she said.

Victoria came back to their table. She told Delia that she wanted to introduce her friend, Ralph Sheldon.

"This is my girlfriend, Delia," Victoria told Ralph.

"I'm glad to meet you, Delia- Victoria talks about you all the time,"

"Are you going to New York tomorrow with Victoria?"

"Yes," replied Delia. "We are driving up there early in the morning and coming back on Sunday," Delia told Ralph.

"You will like New York… there are so many things to do and see."

He gave Delia his phone number to call him any time and told her that he had to leave.

"He's very good looking," Delia told Victoria.

"He's a criminal attorney and very single and available," said Victoria.

"I think I'm going to wait until my problems are solved," Delia told Victoria with a sad laugh.

Peter walked by to say goodbye to her and asked her to call him. Victoria and Delia left the grill at midnight. They said goodbye to each other and promised to see each other in the morning.

CHAPTER 23

SCOTT WAS ALREADY IN BED WHEN SHE GOT HOME. SHE DIDN'T WANT TO wake him up but he was wide awake. He got up and told Delia that they needed to talk tomorrow morning. Delia told him that she was going with Victoria to New York and returning on Sunday.

"I want you to cancel your trip", Scott told her sternly. "You and I need to talk about some very important issues concerning both of us."

"Okay, then I will cancel the trip," she told her husband. She called Victoria and told her that she was unable to go with her to New York.

"Why?" Victoria asked Delia with concern in her voice.

"Scott wants to talk to me," she said.

Delia fixed their breakfast of Vienna sausage and scrambled eggs. Scott came and joined her in the kitchen. They both sat quietly together. He told her that his brother, Steve, was arriving the next day and his parents and his sister were coming on Wednesday. "We have a lot of work to do and I apologize for not spending too much time with you, but we will have a great time when my parents get here," said Scott.

"You can ask Victoria to come and join us then," Scott said to Delia.

Delia exhaled freely again. She thought he was going to say something that she was not wanting him to say.

"Great!" she said. "Victoria and I will clean up the house and buy some new curtains, blankets, rugs, new silver ware and plates," Delia told Scott.

Delia called Victoria right away; she was happy to help her out. When she arrived, Scott was very happy to see her and apologized for cancelling her trip with Delia. He told her that they could all go together when his parents, sister and brother arrived this week. "Sure, we can all go together," said Victoria.

Delia and Victoria sat down and planned the cleaning up of her house. They went to Wal-Mart and bought some rugs, curtains, blankets, silver ware and plates. They went back to the house and started to clean and put up all the new curtains and change the sheets and the blankets. The house had beautiful wooden floors. Victoria polished the wood and they put the new oriental rugs in the living room to match the new couch. Scott was glad to see their large three-bedroom house look wonderful like a model home.

Victoria had dinner with them and helped Delia with the laundry and then left to go back to her place. Later at night, the phone rang and it was Scott's parents. They told Scott they had to postpone their trip on Wednesday for next Monday. His father had to be in court. Scott told them that it was okay. Scott's brother, Steve, arrived the next day. They were all very happy to see each other. They all went out to eat with Victoria and came back to the house and just talked about Scott's school and work. They didn't go to sleep until one o'clock in the morning. Delia had to go back to work and Scott took his brother with him to school. Steve noticed there was something wrong between Scott and his sister in law, Delia. He asked his brother about it but he didn't even say a word. "Your wife looks sick" Steve told his brother. "What's the matter with her?"

"Why don't you ask her yourself?" Scott told his brother.

"If you and your wife are having problems, you need to call mom and dad and tell them not to come," Steve told Scott. "Are you and Delia getting a divorce?" asked Steve.

"We are, but Delia and I haven't sat down yet to talk about it yet," said Scott. "We both want it, Steve. I'm going to Japan and she is moving to Washington D.C. The marriage is over, in all truthfulness. But she is a very strong person. I am selling this house because it has some very bad memories.

"I felt you wanted the divorce, so I'm glad for you, Scott. But Dad and Mom were looking forward for grandchildren from you and Delia," Steve said.

"Delia is not the motherly type," Scott told his brother. "The main reason why I want them to come is so Delia and I can do something together. We hardly have seen each other during the day due to our different schedules. She gets home at five o'clock and I get home at midnight, sometimes at two o'clock in the morning. It has been hard on both of us. There are still some things that I need to confront her with. But I'm going to wait for the right time," Scott told his brother.

"Like when?" asked Steve.

"I can't tell anyone right now," Scott said.

"Let's change the subject. Our sister is arriving tomorrow without her husband!" Steve told Scott.

"Don't worry about Janet; she has a nice husband," said Scott.

Scott and his brother left home early that day to run some errands before their family arrived from Chicago. They called Delia to let her know that they were doing the grocery shopping.

CHAPTER 24

SCOTT COOKED DINNER FOR THEM THAT NIGHT. HE ROASTED A WHOLE chicken with vegetables and baked potatoes. Victoria praised Scott's culinary talents. Delia tried to eat but her stomach was upset sensing that under the normal appearance of their married life together- something was terribly wrong.

Janet, Scott's sister called and told him her flight number and the arrival time. She spoke with Delia for a while and hung up. Janet arrived at six o'clock the next night and everyone, including Victoria, went to meet her at the airport. They stopped to get something to eat before they went home. Delia went to the restroom while Scott and his brother Steve and his sister Janet were talking. Victoria was listening intently to their conversation.

Janet made a remark to Scott about his wife that she didn't look good and seemed very unhappy. Scott told her sister that Delia had been sick for the last two weeks and she just went back to work this past Monday.

"Are you and Delia getting along? She looked terribly tired," Janet commented.

"She has been working very hard and doesn't have time for me," said Scott.

"You have to make time with her otherwise your marriage is going down the drain," Janet said. "She's very beautiful, young, smart and a hardworking person. Both of you need to take a vacation together and spend time together like a married couple. I know it is hard to go back to graduate school while your wife is struggling to support both of you," said Janet to her brother Scott.

"We have a big problem and Delia and I need to resolve it ourselves" Scott told her sister.

"What kind of problem?" his sister asked with deep concern in her voice.

"I can't even say it to you right now. I haven't confronted Delia about it yet. I will wait until you leave," Scott told his sister.

"Okay, I hope you resolve your problems soon. I don't like the way she looks right now. She doesn't look very happy and she looks very skinny. Maybe, before we leave, you can tell me about the problems," Janet said.

"No! No! don't even mention that in front of Delia! She is going to get really mad and leave. I would just leave it alone," said Scott to his sister.

Delia came back to the table and joined them again.

"Are you OK, Delia?" Janet asked with a concerned tone.

"Yes, I'm fine," replied Delia.

Everyone had some tea and coffee and left for home. Delia and Victoria rode together in one car while Scott, Steve and Janet rode in another car. Victoria told Delia that she had very nice in-laws.

"Yes, they are very good people," said Delia. "They are going to be arriving here next Monday. You know, both of his parents are attorneys. They have to finish up his father's trial at court before they come," Delia told Victoria.

"You are very lucky to marry into that sort of family," said Victoria.

"Yes, I feel very lucky," said Delia to Victoria.

"You know, when you went to the bathroom, your sister in law was very concerned about you. Scott told her that he had something to discuss with you, and he didn't want anyone to get involved in it." Victoria told Delia.

Victoria dropped Delia off and they said goodbye to one another. She was very happy to see her sister in law. Janet brought Delia a beautiful pink sweater and an afghan with blue and white colors. She hugged her sister-in-law and warmly thanked her for the thoughtful gifts.

They talked for a while before they went to bed, laughing and remembering their single girls' outing to an all-male dance revue when they first met. Delia shared a bedroom with Janet, while Scott slept in their own bedroom. Steve slept in the guest room. Delia had to get up very early in the morning to leave for work. She told her sister in law that she would come home and have lunch with her. Scott and his brother went to the university together. Delia came to pick up Janet and took her to the Chinese restaurant for lunch.

Janet asked her how she was getting along with her brother, Scott.

"Everything is just fine," said Delia. "He has been very busy at school now because his final exams are coming up and being a graduate student, it's very hard for him. We are very lucky that I have a very good job and I am able to support both of us monetarily. We have our ups and down but we are trying our best to make our marriage work. We don't spend as much time together like we used to. I think this is our biggest problem. Sometimes, I feel that I'm going to lose him but I just don't know what Scott is thinking most of the time," Delia confided to Janet.

"I'm worried about the both of you," said her sister in law. "I told Scott last night that you've lost so much weight and you look unhappy and sick. He told me that you have not been feeling well lately and that you had taken two weeks off from work. He also told me he had something that he wanted to confront you with. He didn't want to discuss it with me. This matter will decide if you and he are going to stay married," Janet said.

"Whatever it is, let him tell you," Delia told her sister in law.

Janet was quiet. After they finished their lunch, Delia took Janet to see her office and meet some people at work. Janet liked her office and the people that worked with Delia. She left work early and took her sister- in-law to the grocery store to do some shopping. Delia told Janet that Scott always did their shopping but now he was too busy at work.

They got home and started cooking a beef roast with potatoes and green beans and French bread. While they were waiting for her husband and Steve, the phone rang and it was their father. He told Delia they wouldn't be able to come because the court case would be dragging on for the next two weeks.

Both Janet and Steve decided to leave on Friday. Delia and Scott enjoyed their visit and especially, Delia, who just loved her sister- in- law. They took them to the airport on Friday morning to fly back to Chicago. They promised each other to stay in touch. Everything was very quiet on the way back to the house. Delia felt the silence to be like a timebomb and Scott held the detonator.

CHAPTER 25

$\mathcal{A}$S SOON AS THEY GOT HOME, SCOTT TOLD DELIA THAT HE HAD TO GO to school to do some work. Delia didn't go back to work but stayed home. She called Victoria to ask her to accompany her to the mall. She came over and picked Delia up. Delia told Victoria that she felt very strange with both of her sister- in- law and brother- in- law around. She felt very guilty with a heavy heart, knowing how she had betrayed her husband and their brother, Scott.

"Shopping is a good cure for a guilty conscience," Victoria said with a friendly hug.

Victoria bought two dresses, pajamas and a suitcase. Delia didn't buy anything. Victoria went and dropped off Delia at her home. Scott was already home and he didn't say anything to her but went straight to bed. Delia slept on the sofa until the next morning. Scott told her that he had to go to Baltimore this weekend and he would be back next Monday. Delia asked him what was happening in Baltimore. Scott told her that they were doing some projects for the university there. Delia told him that she would ask Victoria to come and stay with her.

Scott went to Baltimore and spent the weekend with a young beautiful girl, Gina, whom he met at the university. Gina attended John Hopkins University where she was enrolled in the Medical school. Scott met her at the Maryland University Campus. Scott and Gina met after class for coffee at Starbucks on campus and he was very impressed with her intellectual questions, as well as her long legs and voluptuous figure. Scott had been seeing her recently. The last time Scott was in Baltimore, he spent the night with Gina.

Delia finally found out about Scott's affair one day when she received their telephone bill. She kept seeing this number showing up on the bill. She was beginning to get very suspicious. She looked in Scott's telephone book which he forgot to take with him one day. She saw the name Gina. She dialed the number and Gina's mother answered the phone. She hung up right away. She called her friend, Victoria, to call the number for her and ask the lady where Gina was. Victoria called the number and Gina's mother answered the phone.

Victoria told her that she was Gina's classmate and she was looking for her. Gina's mother told her that Gina used to go to the University of Maryland but that she transferred to John Hopkins University to attend the Medical Nursing School to do more research study. She gave Victoria Gina's telephone number where she could reach her. Victoria thanked her.

She went over to Delia's house and showed her the number.

"That's it! The telephone number my husband has been calling, and I bet you, he is spending the weekend with her." said Delia.

"What are you going to do now?" asked Victoria.

"Nothing! I'm not going to confront my husband now. I will wait until he says something to me," said Delia.

"Delia, I'm going to call the number to see if Gina answers the phone."

"Good idea, Vic," said Delia in a strange voice verging on the edge of hysteria. She was emotionally reeling from the shock of Scott's betrayal and lies. She had never felt jealousy over a rival woman with Scott. But who was she to be hurt or angry when she began the whole cheating cycle? Delia tried to focus on Victoria's calm demeanor and logical actions. Delia was thankful to have an attorney friend who was comfortable playing the love triangle detective role.

Victoria called the number and sure enough, Gina answered the phone and Victoria just hung up. She told Delia that she could hear music and Scott talking in the background.

Delia started crying, "My marriage is all over now. I don't know what I'm going to do. I can't really tell him to leave because I have no proof except the phone bill. What do you think will be the best thing for me to do, Vic?" Delia asked.

"If I were you, I would stay put until he talked to you. In the meantime, just try to be nice to your husband," said Victoria.

CHAPTER 26

*I*T WAS LATE AUGUST AND THE TEMPERATURE IN MARYLAND WAS ABOUT ninety degrees when Scott told Delia that his brother Steve was coming over to help him pack all his belongings. Delia was not completely shocked because she knew what her husband was up to.

She knew this was coming but she didn't know that he was going to do it so soon or in this cowardly way.

"Where are you going Scott?" Delia asked in a high-pitched agitated voice.

"I'm sending all my things to my parents' house in Florida," Scott calmly told Delia.

"You are just going to leave without us talking...without explaining anything to me?" she screeched. She felt like a child who was ready to throw a fit because her father just left her at preschool.

"Do you *really* want to talk about it now?" asked Scott in a sarcastic voice.

"Yes," Delia whimpered like a wounded animal.

"The last twelve months we have not had any sex together. I found out from the clinic that you had an abortion and it was your boss's baby. You didn't even want to tell me about it. I had to find out for myself from searching the drawers. Do you know how painful that was? Do you? Or do you only think of your shallow self? I was going to come to your office and strangle him! I wanted to confront you a long time ago and pack all my clothes and leave. But I loved you too much, Delia, and that is the part you just don't understand!"

Delia, crying, tried to defend herself: "I knew you would figure out that something was wrong. You are the one to blame. How much time did we spend together at home? How many times did you take me out? And how many times have you made love to me? How dare you try to blame me with everything. You have been lying to me about going to Baltimore and your projects. You didn't go to Baltimore for those reasons. You went to sleep with Gina, didn't you…didn't you? answer me Scott! You always do whatever is right for you!" Delia's angry accusatory words fell into an empty hollow space in the room.

"We are separated now, Delia, and I feel this is the best thing for us to do right now," Scott said to Delia. He walked out and closed the door behind him.

Delia felt like he doused her with a cold bucket of foul water and then left her to drown in her own sorrow.

CHAPTER 27

ELIA IMMEDIATELY CALLED HER GIRLFRIEND, VICTORIA. SHE HAPPENED to be in court at that moment. Delia left a desperate message to come by the house after she got off from work. She could not feel anything. She was emotionally drained as if she emptied all her feelings on the field of battle with Scott. Her thoughts bounced around in her head like in an echo chamber. She was separated, soon to be divorced... he was gone...just like that. Somehow, she thought naively, the way her parents had taught her, that love was forever. She went to their bedroom trying to escape from her tortured thoughts in sleep, but the queen-sized bed seemed to laugh at her.

She ran to the couch and cried herself to sleep. She awoke to the stark reality that he was gone forever. Delia glanced at the old grandfather clock in the living room, saw it was after five thirty, and wondered what happened to Victoria. She couldn't still be at her office, maybe she got caught up with the traffic. The doorbell rang and she rushed quickly to the door.

"I'm sorry, I'm so late getting back," Victoria exclaimed. "It's nice and warm in here," Victoria said rushing in the door.

"What's wrong, Delia? Are you crying? "asked Victoria.

"I just had the biggest shock of my life. My marriage is over" said Delia. I can't talk about it right now...I need something to eat to settle my stomach... I will tell you all about it in a moment," Delia said.

She prepared some tea for both of them and went and sat on the sofa across from Victoria.

"Scott and I are separated as of today. I'm crying, upset and mad at myself. My marriage is over and I just don't know what to do. You know, how I always relied on my husband. But now, I am completely lost, I don't know where to start, what am I supposed to do?" cried Delia.

Victoria tried to comfort her.

"Now his brother is going to come down to help him pack," Delia told Victoria.

"What! His brother is coming over? Victoria asked.

"Yes", replied Delia. "Scott is sending all his stuff to his parents in Florida," said Delia.

"I can't believe what's happening here," said Victoria. "Scott is very sneaky- he left everything to the last minute," said Delia.

"What's going to happen to the house?" asked Victoria.

"We are splitting everything" said Delia.

Delia was going to stay at the house until it was sold.

CHAPTER 28

SCOTT'S BROTHER ARRIVED AND HELPED SCOTT PACK EVERYTHING IN Scott's truck and both left on the next day for Florida. Delia was sad and miserable. Scott had a job offer in Japan and he was going to leave the following week from Florida.

She asked Victoria to come and stay with her for a while to make sure that everything was going to be alright. The next day Delia stood in front of the mirror on the side wall. Staring at herself, she saw her face was ghostly white, she felt totally drained, and she was too skinny. Scott went out the door and she was left to look in the mirror. There were dark circles around her eyes from not having enough sleep. Because she had not eaten much over the last three days, her face seemed narrower, and it was taut with lingering tension. Her separation from Scott would change her life forever. She realized now in an unwanted epiphany that she would have to start assessing her entire life, deciding what changes to make.

Scott called her from his parent's house in Florida and told her that he was leaving on the next day for Japan, and she should let his parents know when the house was sold. His harsh business tone was hard for her to swallow, but she had to realize that everything was over now and she needed to go on with her life. Starting all over, for her was hard but she remembered Victoria's wise adage: "What doesn't kill you, will only make you stronger."

The house was sold within a few months. She bought a townhouse in Georgetown, Washington D.C. and hired a lawyer right away to represent her in the divorce. It was hard for her to start all over again.

After fifteen months of separation from Scott, she started to go out and date again to clear some of the lonely thoughts from her mind. She began bar hopping with her friends from work and met different people. She still missed Scott very much. In the back of her mind she was thinking about her parents. They had a perfect lifetime marriage on a beautiful island of Savu. Where had she gone wrong?

She stood in front of the bedroom window in her townhouse and looked out at the view of the river. It was sunny and hot but humid outside. The leafy domes of the trees near the Potomac River were bright green against the azure sky and rising beyond them emerged the stark skyline of Washington D.C.

There is no city like it anywhere else in the world, she thought. She had loved Washington D.C. ever since she had come here as a twenty-year-old with her husband. He had also been addicted to this political, exciting, whirlwind of a city where anything was possible and the sky was the limit, as her mother used to say.

She started to go to happy hours every Thursday, Friday, Saturday and Sunday. She usually arrived home just as the sun was rising at six o'clock in the morning. Now that she was single again, she could go out and meet all kinds of people in the world. But she always had this conservative side to her that she was not brought up to go out every night and enjoy life in the fast lane. Her parents had taught her everything good and they believed in having a good marriage and good family morals like theirs.

Victoria and Delia met to have breakfast at an Italian restaurant called "Little Italy", which served all kinds of Italian and American food. They had the best coffee and wine too. After a very good American breakfast of hash brown, eggs and sausages, they decided to go down to the Smithsonian to browse around this amazing museum. She remembered the last time she was there with Scott. After Victoria and Delia visited the Lincoln Memorial, they indulged in lunch at the Falcon Room, a famous restaurant in downtown, Washington D.C. The place was crowded with politicians and tourists, eating some of the best steaks and salads in the world. They returned home and rested for a while and Victoria went to her place and got her clothes and came back to Delia's house.

"Let's go out and eat at the "Red Rose" restaurant tonight, right next to the "One Ace" club," Delia suggested.

"I always have to go on a diet after I visit you, Delia. How do you stay so skinny?' Victoria asked in a teasing way.

They both dressed and then left for the restaurant. They had made reservations earlier, so although packed with people, when they arrived at seven o'clock, the waitress came and led them straight to their table. They ordered their food and some white wine to sip while waiting for their dinner to arrive.

The house band was playing some jazz music which was very soothing to the soul. After they finished their dinner, they decided to stop at the One Ace club next door. Stylish young people were already dancing on the dance floor. Delia asked Victoria if she was ready to dance the night away.

"You sure have a lot of energy tonight, Delia!" Victoria observed.

After accepting dances with several handsome men, they left the club at midnight. Delia checked her cell phone and saw she had three messages. The first one was from Peter, the second one was from Scott and the third one was from Ralph.

She was too tired to talk to these three men and she decided to talk to them in the morning and went to sleep. The phone was ringing at four o'clock in the morning and she picked it up right away. It was Scott calling from Japan. He asked Delia, how she was and if everything went okay with the selling of the house. "Everything went fine. I transferred your share to your mother's account in West Palm Beach in Florida, and I kept my share," she told Scott.

"Have you found yourself a house?" Scott asked.

"I bought a townhouse in Georgetown, a three-story townhouse."

"Why didn't you buy a house?" asked Scott.

"Maybe I'll buy one later on but I feel comfortable in a townhouse and the neighbors are very nice and quiet."

"Delia, I am calling to let you know that I have met a Korean woman who I plan to marry as soon as our divorce is finalized. I know I will be truly happy, and I wanted to wish you happiness as well."

"Well, thanks for calling to let me know." Delia said numb to the news.

Delia collapsed on her bed and curled up in the fetal position. She was too devasted to cry. She knew in her heart that this was really the end.

CHAPTER 29

ELIA QUIT HER JOB AT THE COUNTY HOUSING AGENCY. SHE DECIDED TO go and sign up for the temporary agency called the Seventh City. She was tired of working at a full-time job. Her first assignment was with an insurance company. She worked there for eight months and they wanted to hire her full time but she didn't want the salary they were offering her. She quit that job and stayed home for a while. She began to feel sorry for herself. She thought about her failed marriage to Scott. She believed her marriage was going to last forever like her parents' bond. She felt she was a failure which really made her very depressed and lonely.

She avoided all her friends and she started to go out every week alone to meet strangers at different night clubs. Delia was descending down a dangerous self-destructive path. She would allow complete strangers to make love to her. She had wanted to rediscover her own self and how to find true love again, but now she found she was little more than a high-end prostitute. Because she was married to Scott when she was eighteen years old, she didn't really enjoy her youth but now that her married life was over, she wanted to fill up that missing gap by enjoying her single life again.

Victoria had been worrying about Delia. She called and called her and finally, she picked up the phone.

"I have been trying to get in touch with you during the last three weeks," Victoria said to Delia. "Are you alright?"

"Yes," she replied. "I'm just lonely, Vic... living without Scott has been really hard for me. I just feel so betrayed, and I was married too young. If I had only listened to my mother. If I had stayed back home, I would have met someone better. If I had just listened to my parents, I wouldn't be miserable the way I am right now," Delia cried.

"Stop feeling sorry for yourself and pull yourself together, Delia!"

"I need to find a job that challenges me and interests me, Victoria."

"Well, take one day at a time. Your first step is to find a job...any job," Victoria stated in her usual matter-of-fact way.

Delia started the next day, as Victoria suggested, to look through the newspaper to find employment. She found an entry level job with a telecommunication company not very far from where she lived.

They asked her to come in for an interview and she was hired right away. She excelled and very quickly climbed higher on the corporate ladder. She had three promotions within a year. She met Mark Kelley who was one of the new managers in her department and he fell in love with her right away. But Delia's past came back to haunt her. She thought to herself, "This is Deja vu all over again." It reminded her of Peter and she refused to get romantically involved at work. She kept Mark instead as a good friend.

Her job was very demanding. She worked overtime every night and arrived home after midnight, but she had chosen to do this every day because she felt she had no life outside her job. She even worked over the weekend. She didn't have a personal life anymore. She was no longer dating and she no longer went out with her friends. Sometimes she would bring work home and work on her computer all night.

Her mother called her one day and asked her to come back home. She explained to her mother that she had a good job now, and she had to go on with her life without Scott. She told her that he had remarried a Korean woman so there were no more false hopes of ever reconciling.

"Delia you have no life, please come back home now," cried her mother.

"No mother, I have a very good job and I am starting a new life. I promise I will write to you every day," Delia told her mother. As soon as they hung up, Delia started to cry out to the empty air: "I really miss my mother! I don't know if I will ever see her again!"

The next day Victoria called and comforted her.

"Everything is going to be alright now-just try to concentrate on your own goals. You have a very good life ahead of you," Victoria reminded Delia.

Victoria and Delia began to enjoy the Washington D.C. night life. The color came back to Delia's cheeks as she let down her long shining hair to ripple over her soft and supple skin. She began to enjoy the company of her friends and the praises of her male admirers once again.

CHAPTER *30*

*T*HE FOLLOWING FRIDAY, HER FRIEND FROM TRINIDAD, ELIZABETH, asked Delia if she wanted to go out with her to that new African club called "Zebra" on California street in downtown Washington D.C.

"Yes, that would be fun! I love that club! I will meet you there at nine o'clock tonight" she told Elizabeth.

The club was crowded with different people from all over the world. Liz already reserved a table for them in the nonsmoking area. Elizabeth was one of Delia's old co-worker and they hadn't seen each other for a very longtime. They were excited to see each other again to share all that had been happening in their lives.

Delia watched the people dancing on the dance floor. The music was so loud that she could hardly make any conversation with anyone inside the club. As she looked straight across from where she was sitting, she saw three distinguished looking men sitting at one table and the fourth one was sitting by himself at an adjacent table. Delia checked him out and he was really good looking. Both Delia and her friend Elizabeth ordered their drinks and Elizabeth said that her boyfriend who was the DJ at the club had already paid for them.

Delia noticed that the man sitting across from her was staring at her. He was about six feet tall, with brown hair and a handsome face. He stood up and her knees trembled when she realized that he was walking over to her to ask for a dance. She was mesmerized by his deep British accent. Delia smiled at him and gracefully stood up to dance with him to the romantic music from the Cameroon in Africa. There was a mutual magnetic attraction between them, perhaps even love at first sight.

"Were you brought up in this country? he asked Delia.

"No, I am from the Savu Island in the South Pacific."

"I was admiring your exotic beauty from a distance but you are even more captivating when I hold you close in my arms. Allow me to introduce myself. I am James Hicks from England."

Their eyes met and they both knew at that moment they would fall madly in love with one another. After their dance, they both went back to their own table and she noticed him ready to leave. Delia stopped him. "Are you leaving now?" she asked. "Yes, our driver is here to pick us up," he said.

He gave Delia his business card and she thanked him. The club closed at three in the morning. "Delia do you want to leave now?" asked Elizabeth. "I know it is only eleven but I need to get up early tomorrow to leave for new Jersey.

"Yes," replied Delia, I am ready to go home too." Everyone said goodbye to one another and Delia returned home. Victoria left her a message to call her when she got home. She made herself some tea and sat down on the couch.

CHAPTER *31*

SHE CALLED VICTORIA BACK AND ASKED HER TO COME OVER AND SPEND the night with her. Victoria arrived and she wanted to know everything about this new guy that she met at the club. Delia took out the business card and she looked at the man's name and what type of work he did. She almost fell on the floor. Her hands were shaking and her voice was trembling.

She yelled out to Victoria. "Oh my God! Vic, just look at this business card. This is the man I met at the club! He is a member of the Parliament in London. My goodness, I have never met a politician from London! He's really good looking, you know the type, tall and handsome. I have never been to London, but maybe this is going to be my reason to go there!"

"Wow, Delia! What an amazing and fortuitous meeting at a nightclub. I can't imagine this happening to a more deserving friend," Victoria responded.

Delia was grinning at Victoria.

"And you look very happy tonight," said Victoria.

"I am" Delia replied. "Guess what I'm going to give him a call," said Delia.

"This late!" said Victoria.

Delia started dialing the hotel number and asked for James Hicks. The operator transferred her call over to his room and he picked up the phone right away. "Good evening, Mr. Hicks. My name is Delia, the girl you met at the club tonight," she told him.

"Please forgive me for calling at this late hour but I do believe it is earlier in London. It is a great honor to meet a very important politician like you," Delia said.

He laughed at her and told her that he was glad to meet someone as pretty as her.

"As a matter of fact, Miss Delia, I would like to share dinner with you in Georgetown on Saturday night. I will pick you up with my driver at 7:00. Please message me your address. I am looking forward to furthering our acquaintance," he told Delia.

They said good night and hung up.

"Victoria! Guess what? I am going on a very special date tomorrow! Will you help me find just the right outfit to wear in the morning at the Georgetown mall?"

She joined Victoria for breakfast at Molly's in Georgetown and they went to the mall to buy an outfit for her to wear that night. She found a beautiful pink dress with a low-cut back. She tried it on and it fit her like a silken glove. She went and had her hair done at the salon. She looked exquisitely beautiful. She took a long nap and she didn't even realize that James had left her a message on the phone. He wanted her to call him as soon as she got home.

She called him back right away. He asked her if they could meet at six o'clock instead of at seven. She looked at the clock; it was almost five o'clock in the evening.

The townhouse was very neat and beautifully decorated. These things came naturally to Delia. As she walked up the stairs, she looked at the two Russian crystal vases filled with fresh gardenia flowers. She straightened her townhouse up and then took a shower, telling herself that her raised vital signs did not mean that she was anticipating James' arrival. She was in a quandary about what to wear. Chances were, James would be wearing a nice conservative suit because he was English and a politician.

Delia didn't want to appear too dressy, but she wanted to look good. She settled for the pink dress she bought from the mall with the low-cut back and spaghetti straps, and black low heel shoes. She wore a simple white pearl necklace with her hair combed back. As a last-minute inspiration, she placed a gardenia behind her right ear.

James really was a stranger in her life and this could be just a one-night affair which she didn't really like, but she wanted to experience how to fall in love again. She inhaled deeply. Maybe an evening with the English politician would convince her how different their lives were, an island girl and a politician. She felt her pearl necklace, hoping that she was not overdressed.

When she opened the door, she hung on to the doorknob to keep from falling. James Hicks stood there looking like a million-dollar politician with a brown suit, light brown shirt, and brown dress shoes. His light brown hair was neatly combed, his square jaw cleaned-shaven.

"You look beautiful," he said with genuine awe.

"You look great too!" Delia replied. "Are you ready to tour the city?" she asked.

He just grinned at her and led her like royalty to his waiting limousine. He told his driver to take them to the Crazy Horse restaurant in Georgetown.

It was beautiful inside the restaurant and they both sat down at their table and ordered their food. While they were waiting for their dinner to be served, he told Delia they just arrived from Japan yesterday morning. It was a very long flight. "How did you end up at the Zebra club last night"? Delia asked.

"Our driver who knows all the D.C. hotspots took us there," he replied.

After they were done with their dinner, they went dancing at the Rumors night club. It was packed with people. They found an empty table, sat down, and ordered specialty cocktails. They were staring into each other's eyes speechless for what seemed like an eternity and finally James broke the silence.

"You are very attractive and you have the most beautiful eyes," James told Delia. "You're not bad looking yourself' Delia commented.

"Would you care to join me for a nightcap in my hotel room?" James asked with his compelling Queen's English.

"Yes, what lady would not be delighted to end the evening in this way with you?" Delia softly replied.

They went to his hotel and had breakfast and slept off the alcohol for three hours before they had lunch. James did not want to leave Delia but she told him that she needed to go home and change her clothes, and then she would come back to see him.

"I don't live too far from your hotel- actually it is an easy walking distance," she told him.

"I want to come with you to your house," he said.

He escorted her with great dignity down the sidewalk to her front door. James was amazed to see how beautiful the town house was. When he picked her up earlier, he had not gone inside. "Nice place," he said.

It's about ten years old" Delia said. "It's very well built and the neighbors are not lunatics!" said Delia with a little grin.

"It seems quite comfortable," James replied. Touching the fireplace brick and pointing to the pictures above the wooden mantle, he indirectly inquired, "and these must be your parents,". Delia nodded. "You look like both of your parents," he said.

"Thank you. They are wonderful humble parents who have given me much love," replied Delia.

"Who are these people?" he asked, gesturing to the other frames.

"There's Nikki, my girlfriend who lives in New York. And Victoria a federal prosecutor. They are both single and determined to meet Mr. Right."

"And who are these two gentlemen?" he politely asked.

"They are Scott, my ex-husband and Peter my ex boyfriend," she told James. "They're both very handsome men!" Delia just nodded in agreement.

After Delia prepared a light dinner, they enjoyed cocktails and conversations until midnight. James ended up spending the night there in Delia's guest room. Early in the morning, Delia accompanied James at his hotel. He told Delia that he was leaving on Monday for London. On Sunday, he called Delia to say goodbye. Just as the conversation was ending, he told Delia to come and see him in London. "I will," she told him. They said goodbye and hung up.

CHAPTER 32

*D*ELIA'S LIFE WAS GOING IN A VERY GOOD DIRECTION NOW. SHE HAD BEEN going to the gym with her girlfriend every day. She looked healthy and well. She had so many new projects at work that she practically became a workaholic.

One day, her longtime girlfriend, Nikki, from New York called. She wanted to come and spend two weeks of vacation with her. Delia told her that she would be very happy to have her. She arrived on Friday evening. They didn't go out anywhere but spent the whole evening just doing some catching up concerning their individual lives and the good old days. Nikki asked Delia if she believed in fortune tellers.

"No, I don't believe in those people. Actually, we have two well-known Fortunetellers who work out of their homes just up the street. Why do you ask? Do you believe in what they say?" asked Delia.

"Yes, I do believe in what they tell me," replied Nikki. "They have told me things that really have happened. For example, my trip over here. She saw that a long time ago. She also told me that you and Scott were having problems and your marriage would end up in divorce" Nikki told Delia

"Really?' said Delia. "Well, since we don't have anything planned for tonight... Let's go and see Mrs. White! I'm very curious what she's going to tell me," said Delia.

They dressed and walked over to the home of Mrs. White, the Fortuneteller. When they arrived, there were two people ahead of them.

"Let's go and see Maria on the other side," Delia told Nikki. They both went to see Maria and she was available.

Delia asked Nikki to go first. Maria charged twenty dollars for fifteen minutes, forty dollars for half an hour and forty-five for one hour.

Maria was a stunning elderly woman with a middle eastern accent and beautiful green eyes. She was wearing a long black dress and dangling silver earrings. She had long black hair with blond highlights swept back into a bun. She read Nikki for fifteen minutes and then it was Delia's turn. Delia was scared at first to have her do this. Maria was a renowned psychic and Delia was afraid of what Maria was going to tell her.

"Hello," she smiled as she shook Delia's hand. "I'm Maria and welcome to my house," she said.

"I really appreciate you seeing me tonight. Should I be wondering if I should trust you?"

"Relax Delia. Would you like some herbal tea? I will be right back. Make yourself comfortable," she said.

Delia looked around the living room. She noticed a beautiful yellow curtain and a pretty white couch noticeably in the middle. The couch looked wobbly and Delia thought it was unreliable to sit on. Delia picked the red chair across from her as she waited for Maria to come back.

"Sit down Delia. I just brought a tray out so the tea is hot" Maria sat across from her. Maria poured the tea in two mismatched cups and saucers.

Maria's face was pretty and soft with little lines on her forehead and around the corner of her green eyes. She was in her sixty odd years. Delia noticed beautiful rings made from crystals and a crystal bracelet when she offered her the cup of tea. Comfortable with herself, she settled back and looked straight at Delia. "You are here for a psychic reading too?" she asked Delia.

She was very nervous and Maria calmed her down.

"Take a deep breath Delia, and breathe in and out slowly.

Finally, Delia was calmed down. She asked Maria to give her an hour reading and tell her the most important things that are coming or going to happen in her life.

"I see that you are going to take a trip outside the United States and I see this man who is very tall and handsome and very intelligent. It looks like he's in a very powerful job. He is not an American. You've met this man before and you will see him again on this trip that you are just about to take. You will leave Washington D.C. and move to Europe," she told Delia.

"Wait a minute, I don't want to move to Europe, and I have a very good job here. I just don't believe that I'm going to live in Europe," Delia protested.

"Don't interrupt me until I'm done with your reading," Maria warned Delia. "You will go first and visit Europe and then you will be back again and then you will be moving there. Your luck is in Europe," she told Delia.

"Okay, Maria, can you please tell me what part of Europe that I will be living in?" "England! I see England" she said. "The man you are going to marry is English," Maria said.

Delia was amazed and astounded. Maria continued her reading in a matter of fact but mystical way.

"Your health is very good... just prepare yourself and look forward to all the good things that are coming to you," she told Delia.

"I know the man you are talking about!" Delia exclaimed.

Where does he come from?" asked Maria.

"England, he's a member of the British parliament," Delia told Maria.

"I saw that. You will see him again," Maria said. "You really like this man."

"Yes, I do." Delia affirmed.

"He likes you a lot and he's hoping that he's going to see you again. He is the one you are going to be settling down with," Maria said to Delia.

Delia just couldn't believe what this woman was telling her but she would wait to see what destiny brought. Victoria met them over at Maria's office. She wanted a fifteen minutes reading. Afterwards, they all went back to the house and tried to swallow everything that the fortune teller told them. Delia told them that she was going to keep her mouth sealed until the time comes.

Nikki told them what Maria told her and she believed everything she told her. The fortune teller told her that she was going to have a new job which was true. She also told her that she would meet a wealthy man who would marry her, but that her marriage wouldn't last for a very long time. "I haven't met the wealthy man yet," she told Delia and Victoria. They all started laughing again!

Victoria told them what Maria told her. "She told me that I'm going to move out in three months. I will meet someone new and we would live together and that I would have a child with this man. I asked her if this man would marry me, and she told me "No." I didn't really like that answer," Victoria said.

Victoria shared with her friends why she thought some clairvoyants can see into the future. "I don't think we can change our destiny. Before we were born, God has already planned our destiny. Let's wait and see the outcome of her readings."

They didn't want to go out on the town that night. They all went to the grocery store and bought some fish and chicken. Delia barbecued on her patio, Niki cooked some corn and Victoria prepared potato salad. They had Italian rum cake for dessert. They all sat around the table and ate their dinner with two bottles of wine. After their dinner, they played monopoly, boggle and scrabble.

"This wine is really boggling my brain!" Delia abruptly announced ... I think I just saw a vision of my future husband," she said laughing with the others.

CHAPTER 33

ELIA GOT UP THE NEXT MORNING WITH A SLIGHT HEADACHE AND A feeling of expectation in her heart. She made a cup of tea and lazily brought in the newspaper from the porch. "What is this?" she suddenly exclaimed. There on the front page of the Washington Post, she saw a picture of James shaking the hand of the President. She devoured the article and discovered that James and other British Parliament members were staying at the British Embassy in Washington D.C. She waited at home all day hoping that he would call. That night about nine o'clock she tried to call James. It was hard to suppress her rising excitement and it was even harder to reach him.

Finally, she got through to him. He was glad to hear from her. Delia told him she saw his picture on the Washington Post and the newspaper article mentioned where they were going to be. He apologized profusely that his butler forgot to contact Delia to tell her that he would not be able to see her due to their tight schedule. He promised that he would make it up to her whenever she visited London. They said goodbye and hung up. Delia was happy to talk to him.

Delia continued to be very busy at work. Suddenly, she had the feeling that she could wait no longer to see James again. She decided to take a trip to England in the fall. She called the travel agency and booked her flight for November second. She didn't tell Victoria about her plan. Nikki went back to New York and promised to keep in touch with them. Delia tried to finish most of her projects at work before she took a ten-day vacation to London.

About one week before she left for London, she finally told Victoria about her planned trip to London. She was excited for her and reminded her about the fortune teller's romantic prediction.

The next night Delia was awakened by the phone ringing and she picked it up right away. It was James calling from England. She was encouraged to hear his voice. Delia told him that she was flying over to England in just one week. He was very surprised and happy.

She told him that she was going to stay with some friends in Kensington. He told her to give him a call when she got to London. They said good bye. After that phone call, she couldn't go back to sleep. She kept thinking about the fortune teller, Maria, and how amazing she was. What she told her was beginning to come true.

CHAPTER 34

SHE CALLED VICTORIA AT 3 AM.
"I talked to James a while ago. As a matter of fact, he woke me up," Delia told Victoria.

"Really!" Victoria replied. "And you just woke me up too, my dear friend."

"I was so excited to hear his voice with his British accent. I told him about my trip and he couldn't believe that I was arriving so soon. I am just amazed about the fortune teller. She has this magical gift. It is incredible. What she told me is coming true. She told me that James would call me before I left for London."

"What did James have to say?" she asked.

"Nothing important but he's really looking forward to my arrival," Delia told Victoria.

Victoria had news to share too about the man that Maria saw with her.

"He called yesterday and told me that he bought a house on Connecticut avenue," said Victoria.

Delia interrupted her. "Hey! Vic, that is where all the wealthy people in Washington D.C. live!"

"I didn't know that! all I know is that he asked me to move in with him," said Victoria sounding lovestruck.

"Are you serious?" responded Delia. "That sounds exciting and just as Maria the fortune teller predicted!"

She also told me that I would have two children with him, and this is the most interesting part, that he would never marry me," said Victoria.

"What kind of craziness is that?" asked Delia.

"You tell me," Victoria said. "I asked Maria why he wouldn't marry me. And she explained that this man had many women who wanted to marry him in the past but he didn't want to marry any of them because he's very wealthy. He doesn't believe in marriage but, she also said, who knows, he might change his mind and marry you!"

"Wow Vic, I can't believe that this is actually happening to you too. I am very happy for you. Finally, you've met someone who is going to love you forever and I've known you for a very long time, and I know the kind of guys who hung around you. You know, they just broke your heart and left you in the cold. You've called me in the middle of night crying or just to have long talks, "said Delia. "When are we going to meet him?" asked Delia.

"I will call him in the morning after we finally get some sleep and we can go to his house," she said.

"What is his name, Vic" asked Delia.

"His name is Christopher Baron, a very proper name!"

CHAPTER 35

$\mathcal{V}$ICTORIA CALLED CHRISTOPHER THE NEXT MORNING AND ASKED HIM IF they could come to visit him and he accepted her invitation. He was happy to see her. She introduced Delia to him. He was about six feet tall, slender, blonde hair, blue eyes and very handsome. He was in his late forties.

You are beautiful Delia!" Christopher commented. Do you have a boyfriend? he asked.

"I'm still looking," Delia responded. Victoria laughed out loud.

Victoria and Delia stopped at the Connected Café for a bite to eat before heading home.

"You are very lucky Vic, to meet someone really nice. How did you meet him?" asked Delia.

"I called his office and said that I was looking for someone to come and hook up my computer for me. The justice department has been dealing with his company for years and as a matter of fact, they have a government contract with us. They sent a computer technician over to my office to install my computer. I wasn't there when he came but my secretary was there. She showed him where to install the computer.

He hooked everything up and he made sure that everything was working right. He left his business card with Irene, my secretary. I returned to my office after a very long time at the courthouse. I turned on my computer, and it didn't even come on. I called Irene right away and asked her about the problem that I was having with my computer. She came and tried to help me out but all was in vain. She told me right away that the installer left his business card. I asked her to call him for me and she left him a message to call me back concerning my computer," she explained to Delia.

"Their secretary called Irene back, and told her that the installer was on another call and she didn't think he was coming back to the office that day. While the secretary still was talking to Irene, Christopher, the owner of the company happened to walk by and he overheard their conversation. He asked Susan, their secretary, what was going on and who was on the phone. She told him an attorney from the justice department had a complaint about the quality of their company's service.

She gave the phone over to Chris and he apologized to Irene and he asked to pass on his apologies to the justice attorney, who was of course me. And that's how it all started."

"Great story, Vic," said Delia

"Thanks, Delia," replied Victoria. Chris made sure in person that my computer was installed properly and that is how God planned for us to meet!" she said to Delia.

They both burst out with laughter.

"He called me up one week later and asked me out for dinner. He told me that he doesn't usually do that," Victoria explained to Delia.

"What did he mean?" Delia asked.

"Oh, you know, asking women out who are business clients. I just couldn't believe that someone like that would be attracted to me. Strange thoughts began creeping in my mind like what if this was just a one-night stand and like…I don't want to be *that* kind of girl…and like…I'm not going to call him; he probably has too many girlfriends. I was too tired to do anything that night. I took my shower and went to sleep. He called my office two days later, I went out to dinner with him, and I have been seeing him ever since then," Victoria told Delia.

"I'm so happy for you and let's both hope that these two men, Christopher and James, are going to love us forever. They both burst out laughing again.

"Vic, you should thank the fortune teller!" Delia told Victoria.

"Yes, that's for sure" replied Victoria.

CHAPTER 36

THEY BOTH RETIRED TO BED. DELIA COULDN'T GO SLEEP. SHE KEPT ON turning and thinking about her big trip to London. She thought about James and how exciting it was to be with him and spend time with him. But she was not really happy that she would only see him for a very short time and that she would be wondering the whole time when she would see him again. These troubling thoughts kept bothering her. She often wondered why God brings certain people into our lives at certain moments. Delia assumed that these people must have something to learn about love and relationship from each other. She also realized that evening was Tuesday and she had only one day before her trip to London.

She didn't get up until eleven o'clock in the morning and then she took her shower and fixed her breakfast. She checked everything in her suitcase to make sure that she hadn't forgotten everything. She bought two sweatshirts for James. She figured that it was always cold in London. Victoria and Delia went to the Bistro and ordered some sea food dishes and some white wine for a farewell dinner. The food was delicious and the wine as well. Victoria bought her dinner that night.

"I wish you could come with me to London, Vic," Delia said

"Maybe I will go with you next time," she said. "This is your time alone with James"

Delia and Victoria had some more tea and talked about Maria, the clairvoyant. Victoria suggested that they invite Maria to come to the house or take her out to dinner.

"That's a good idea, Victoria." But you know, Delia pondered out loud, those fortune tellers are very funny people. They don't socialize with their own clients or any outside people. I read this in a magazine."

"Oh, that's interesting," Victoria commented.

"The magazine article said that they prefer to be by themselves or with their own families," Delia explained. "I guess they like to keep their gifts to themselves.".

"We've prosecuted several of them due to fraud but that doesn't mean they are all bad people," Victoria told Delia. "But I think we should always be suspicious when they say certain things and then they demand too much money for their advice." "I am a very logician person and fortunetellers; psychic predictions and telepathy don't fit into my life style" Victoria told Delia

"Fraud! Really? What did you feel about Maria?" Delia asked Victoria.

"She hasn't really asked us for a large amount of money but we should be careful anyway," she said.

CHAPTER 37

ELIA GOT UP EARLY THAT MORNING AND SHE CHECKED HER SUITCASES one more time to make sure she didn't forget anything. She pulled out her passport and her visa and checked if everything was okay. She even checked her flight tickets to see that "round trip" was stamped on them. She called her friends in London to tell them that she was leaving that evening. She also told them her flight number and the arrival time. Victoria picked Delia and then drove her to the because the traffic was heavy and it was raining hard outside. Victoria took her time driving on the freeway.

It was five o'clock when they arrived at the airport. Delia got out with her suitcase while Victoria went and parked the car. She went into the main terminal and checked in her suitcase and got her boarding pass. She went and sat down on the chair waiting for Victoria. There were many people going to London. She saw the long line waiting to board the plane. Finally, Victoria arrived and she wished Delia a safe journey and asked her to call when she arrived to London.

The announcer said on the loudspeaker that flight 778 leaving for London was ready for departure and that all passengers should report to gate four. Delia stood up and hugged Victoria and they said goodbye. Delia went and stood in line with the rest of the passengers going to London. Everyone started boarding the British Airways plane while the air hostess checked everyone's boarding tickets. Delia was happy with her seat in the plane. She was seated near the window near the tail of the plane. She had a nice view of the sky and the clouds. It was raining heavily outside. She could see the rain drops on top of the left wing which splashed the window as well. She sat next to a pleasant and good-looking man. The plane took off from the airport for London. He introduced himself to Delia.

"My name is Michael Gavin," "What is your name?" he asked.

"I'm Delia," she said.

He asked Delia if she lived in Washington D.C. They had a very long conversation while they were waiting for their dinner to be served. He told Delia that he was an attorney in Washington D.C. and he was going for vacation to London, Paris, and Italy. "How about you?" he asked.

"I'm going to London for ten days," Delia replied.

"Have you been to London before?" he asked.

"No, this is my first time," Delia told him. "How about you, have you been to London?" she asked.

"Many times," he told Delia. "I love London and you will love London too. It's a beautiful city and they have many old buildings and quite a history. England reminds me of an old mother who has birthed many countries, including America."

"Where are you staying in London?" he asked Delia.

"I'm going to stay with some friends in Kensington," Delia responded.

"That's a very beautiful area. Mainly for the rich people. That's where Princess Diane lives," said Michael.

Finally, their dinner arrived. They had traditional English "bangers and mash" with garden peas and tea with a Scottish shortbread for dessert. It took them five hours to fly from Dulles airport to Heathrow airport in London. Delia dozed off to sleep right after dinner.

She awoke when the light streamed in the window and noticed the plane was flying very low over Ireland and across the English Channel and she knew right away that they were just about to land. She heard the pilot make an announcement to prepare for landing at Heathrow airport. The stewardess reminded them to make sure they had their passports ready and their customs papers completed.

The airport really looked huge from the air, as they ready to land in one of the busiest airports in the world.

There were many people coming into the airport that morning.

There were different kinds of people, different colors, different languages, and different clothes.

After claiming her luggage, Delia caught a cab to take her to Kensington, where she was going to be staying with her friends. It was raining when she finally arrived by taxi in this upscale neighborhood with Georgian and Victorian townhouses interspersed with fashionable clothing shops and elegant bakeries. The chilly late winter rain seemed to suit her mood. She had slept nearly all the way across the Atlantic.

She climbed the stately stairs of the Kensington townhouse and rang the doorbell. Their housekeeper came and greeted Delia at the door. Loraine and her son Max were happy to see Delia. Loraine was a private English doctor who made house calls every day.

They both were delighted to see a familiar face from back home. Loraine's ex-husband lived in Washington D.C. and Max was their only child. Delia brought some gifts from Keith. They were very happy to receive them. The last time Delia had seen Max, he was only ten years old, but now he is matured. They all went out to dinner that night at Ye Ole Cheshire Cheese in the oldest part of London. Afterwards, they took a taxi to walk in Kensington Park about two blocks away from Princess Diane's home. They returned to Lorraine's 19th century brown stucco townhouse and Delia, jetlagged, went straight to bed in the cozy guestroom. Loraine had chosen to decorate the bedroom with Laura Ashley designed rose printed curtains and matching sheets and comforter on the four-poster bed. The Victorian vanity had a silver mirror and brush. Delia felt at home. She thought about James but she was too tired to even call him. She decided to call him in the morning when she felt refreshed and vibrant.

CHAPTER 38

As soon as Delia awoke to the busy street sounds of London, she called James. He told her that he knew she arrived yesterday morning, and he had waited to hear from her.

"I was really tired yesterday. I went out to eat with my friends and went straight to bed afterwards," Delia told James.

I would like for you to come here to the House of Commons to see me, Delia. I'm very excited to see you again," he said.

"I feel the same way, James," replied Delia.

"I want you to take the tube from Kensington and get off at the House of Commons. I will be waiting at the entrance," James told Delia.

The first thing Delia did was to get her token so she could buy her all-day pass which cost one British pound. She boarded the train, "the tube", from a platform deep below Kensington station. It was packed with people. It had a narrow tunnel compared to the Washington D.C. metro rails. She looked at the tunnel and felt anxious. She had this strange feeling it was going to cave in or something horrible was going to happen.

She remembered reading that the British have had this train system for a very long time but they hadn't done much modernizing. She got off at her stop and she decided to walk faster to meet James. They met at the St. Stephen gate which is the main entrance to the House of Commons, and they were happy to see each other. They went behind a column and discreetly hugged each other. He asked Delia to follow him. They went through the St. Stephen hall to the House of Commons chamber. Inside, the House of Commons had simple green backed benches with plain wooden floors.

The speaker and Prime Minister sat in the center of the chamber from where the speaker kept order in the room. The government MP sat on the right and the opposition to the left. The front benches were reserved for government Ministers and the opposition shadows. The Prime Minister and the leader of the opposition party faced off across their dispatch box in the center of the room. They were just getting ready to start their session and James left Delia where she could observe the lively political debates. James was proud to represent his Northern Yorkshire district. He took their issues to heart.

When the debate was over, James came and got Delia again and they went and had lunch in the dining area.

They both ordered fish and chips with vinegar. James then took her to their house bar where everyone went, including the House of Lords. James gave her an English ale which tasted nasty and bitter to her. She couldn't even swallow it! He told her he was going to his office and she should wait for him to give her a ride back to his hotel.

James told her that he usually stayed in London until Friday and then he would go back to his constituency. The hotel was very old but the inside was very modern. He asked Delia if she was hungry. "Yes", she replied. He ordered some steaks and salad and a bottle of red wine. The dinner arrived but Delia only nibbled on salad. They talked about how amazing it was when they met at the Zebra club for the first time.

"Here we are in London together," he told Delia. "I have thought about you many times and I have often wished you were here with me in London," he told Delia. It was eleven o'clock at night and Delia told James that she wanted to go home.

He stopped her from leaving and he asked her to spend the night with him. She told him that she needed to call her friends and let them know that she would be spending the night with her friend.

James was already in the bedroom and he called her. "Delia are you coming to bed with me? The choice is up to you."

CHAPTER 39

SHE WAS STANDING NEAR THE DOOR OF THE BEDROOM, IN THE ELEGANT drawing room. Desire flooded through her entire body, pounding through her heart, awakening every cell with tingling life. There was silence between them for long seconds, while her mind raced with confusion.

She swallowed really hard, not entirely sure what word would pour out from her mouth. She escaped to the bathroom, closed the door behind her and leaned against it. She looked at herself in the mirror, touched her face, her hair and concentrated on things that physically defined her.

Those deep dark desires lingered in her heart. She didn't like it, knowing her body would override her reason. But she couldn't help how much she wanted James. How much she wanted to share his bed. Then she stopped thinking, opened the door, inhaled deeply and walked into the bedroom to the British politician, and let him make love to her.

"I want you very much and I couldn't wait to get you into bed, but we have the rest of our lives to make love," James whispered tenderly.

She slid her arms around his neck, pulled him down so that he was lying on top of her. They hungrily touched each other in intimate places, and swiftly his passion soared. She felt sudden heat coming through her, and she clung to him, loving him so much, then her legs went around his back as he entered her, and she cried out as if she was taken by surprise.

This thrilled him, and when she began to thrust her body vigorously against his, he thought he would explode with excitement. Within a second, they were moving in unison; they found their perfect rhythm. It was a rhythm that swiftly increased, and the faster they moved the more excited they both were. And as she calmed in ecstasy, she cried out his name and he called out hers a split second later, telling her over and over again how much he loved her.

After they had calmed down, they took a shower, stood under the running water, and wrapped in each other arms. It was as if they were unable to pull apart. But they finally did so, and Delia went into the bedroom to dry her hair and brush it into shape. She was still wrapped in a towel, putting on a few touches of make up when James came back into the bedroom and quickly got dressed. Then he sat down in a chair and watched her, overjoyed that he had found her.

Yes, he had found his true love in this unstable world, and he felt very lucky. This island girl was a perfect fit in every possible way. They were in tune with each other. He knew he was already entrapped and longing to be with her, to hold her in his arms again and again forever.

She knew he loved her with great devotion, and she loved him back, in her own way.

They made love all night and all morning alone together. He told her that he loved her very much and she told him the same thing. They both couldn't believe it... but she told him that fate had brought them together again.

"You know, Delia sighed as she snuggled closer to his heart, when I met you, I just knew we were soul mates. I never dreamt that I was ever going to come to London but God sent you over to America to bring me here to you. I always think of you and I am always wondering if you are thinking about me. But I believe that there is always a reason why things happen."

James replied with sincere tenderness: "Darling Delia, when I saw you for the very first time in the night club, I thought you were the most beautiful woman I ever met. You looked like a fashion model. There was something about your eyes. Yes, you have the most beautiful eyes. I was watching you the whole night at the club, the way you walked, the way you danced so gracefully. I thought to myself, where did this beautiful woman come from? One of my gentleman companions even commented on your magnetic beauty when you first entered the club. We were all looking at you. But here you are in my arms and I yearn to keep you here forever."

The first night they spent together they didn't go to sleep but talked all night. The next day, James didn't go to work but spent the whole day with her. They spent most of their time just lying in bed, holding each other, enjoying heart to heart conversations.

They lived so far away from each other. They both knew that long distance relationships did not always work out, but they both tried to enjoy each other while they could. James had to go back to his constituency in the evening but promised Delia that he would be back on Saturday afternoon to be with her.

CHAPTER 40

A T FOUR O'CLOCK HE LEFT HER IN HIS HOTEL AND HE DROVE UP TO Yorkshire which was about a three-hour and fifty- minute drive from London. He decided that Delia should stay with him until she returned to Washington D.C. Delia thanked him and then took a cab to pick up her luggage from her friend's house. She told James that she would be waiting for him on Saturday when he returned.

Delia called Victoria from their hotel room when she returned from Kensington. She was happy to hear from Delia. "Are you enjoying London?" Victoria asked.

"I am really enjoying my trip in so many ways," said Delia.

"How are you doing, Victoria?"

"I spent the night with Chris at his new house. I am waiting for you to return so I can pack my things and move in with him."

"I'm very happy for you," Delia replied.

Victoria then asked Delia about James.

"He invited me to come to the House of Commons and meet him there. He took me inside the Parliament while they were in session. Afterwards, we went to his hotel and I ended up spending the night with him and it was really hard for us to leave each other. He told me to go and get all my things and come and stay with him at his hotel until I leave."

"Wow! Delia, that's really great! I'm glad that he finally had some time with you. A long distant relationship is always hard," said Victoria.

"That's very true," replied Delia. "He left this afternoon to go home and he will come back tomorrow afternoon. These international calls are expensive. We can share all the juicy details when I return home. I will see you soon."

"I can't wait. In the meantime, enjoy your handsome politician!"

Delia took a shower and dressed in casual clothes. She walked across the street to a little café that was packed with tourists and locals. She stood in line for half an hour until the waitress came and led her to her table. She ordered Belgium waffles and some sausages, orange juice and a cup of tea.

While she waited to be served, she looked outside at the red double decker buses and the black English taxi cabs rushing by in a busy blur and then she admired the beautiful view of the hotel where she was staying with James across the street. It was an old building but the architect of the building designed it to be built like a palace with pure white marble and French windows. After she had her breakfast, she went back to the hotel and unpacked all her clothes and pulled out the sweatshirt she was going to give James as a gift for the damp foggy winter weather. The phone rang and it was James. He told her that he was on his way back and he would be there in twenty minutes.

CHAPTER 41

ELIA WAS SO HAPPY TO SEE JAMES AGAIN. HE BARELY HAD HIS SUIT COAT off before they began to kiss each other passionately. He made love to her again and again. It was steaming hot. They started in the bed and ended up in the bathtub.

Famished after their vigorous workout, they dressed and went out on the busy streets of London to have lunch at James' favorite pub, the White Swan.

"Oh! Delia, I love you very much and I can't resist making love to you. I want you to stay in London. Please don't go back to Washington D.C.," James pleaded.

Delia just kept quiet and didn't even say a word. She stayed silent for a very long time. Then she told James, "If you want me to stay in London, I have to find myself a job, unless you are thinking of marrying me," she told James.

"Delia, I will buy your ticket to return to me in a month. You can end your job, sell or rent your townhouse, say good-bye to your friends in D.C. and come live with me. I want to introduce you to my family at Christmas in Yorkshire and take you to meet my cousins on the French Riviera for the New Year. We can plan our wedding and honeymoon for the end of July when the Parliament is not in session. Then I will whisk you away to the romantic isle of Capri for our honeymoon,

"Well I don't think I can resist you or your romantic offer. Yes, dear James, I will marry you but first I must meet your family for their approval. After all, I am just an island girl from Savu Island. Will they welcome me and possibly our mixed-race grandchildren into their English family tree?"

"Of course, Delia. It is a bit of a whirlwind romance, to put it mildly, but all of my family realize that I have been waiting for just the perfect match. They will see right away that is you that I have been waiting for, my darling Delia." He blushed slightly when he realized the old couple seated next to them in the pub were listening to every passionate word he breathlessly spoke. A public display of affection, even in a pub, was frowned upon by the upper English class.

Unaware of this protocol, Delia sensuously stroked his hand as she told him how much she looked forward to spending Christmas and New Year with him and his family.

That very afternoon, he took Delia to visit a jewelry store in Knightsbridge to be fitted for an engagement ring and wedding band. James flattered Delia by telling her that her slender delicate hands were like those that belong to the ladies of the highest British nobility. He chose a ring for Delia that was set with deep blue sapphires and sparkling diamonds in the shape of an island flower. She gasped when the jeweler mentioned discreetly the total number of carats in the beautiful ring. The jeweler also gave them their first wedding gift, a set of gold-plated tiny spoons to be used at English High Tea.

CHAPTER 42

O N SUNDAY, SHE PROUDLY WORE HER ENGAGEMENT RING AS JAMES introduced her to the National Art Gallery on Trafalgar Square. Delia loved the painting by Leonardo DaVinci called the *Madonna of the Rocks*. Mother Mary was royally seated in a rock cave. She was reaching out her one arm to bless her Christ baby while her other arm was embracing his cousin, John the Baptist. What was mysterious to Delia was that the cave was open in the back and revealed a beautiful blue in the distance. Delia was also drawn to the Island Art exhibit, featuring works by Paul Gauguin. She felt at home when she viewed paintings which depicted a white plumeria tucked into the black wavy hair of a brown skinned woman, ripe mangoes painted in bright pinkish orange, and voluptuous large bodies lounging on sand by azure seas. She did not feel at home in the dark wooden rooms of the gallery where the walls were hung with oil painted portraits of rich aristocrats looking down on her. She felt they were smirking at her-not really smiling- and they looked unnatural dressed in their lacey high collared shirts surrounded by gawdy ornate frames. No, Delia did not feel at home in the rooms and halls of these stuffy paintings. For a moment, she doubted that she could feel at home in James' circle of high society Parliament members.

James jolted her out of her musing. "Delia, come with me to see my favorite landscape paintings. Look, here are Constable's pastoral paintings of the English countryside! This is what you will see when you visit my manor house in Yorkshire."

"Oh, how lovely," Delia sighed with relief, as she looked at the spreading English oak trees arching over the heath, with shepherds watching their sheep grazing near babbling streams.

"I could live there," Delia said as she dreamed into this landscape.

"Come, Delia, let's have tea and scones and cucumber and cheese sandwiches in the Gallery café before my driver takes us for our visit to the world-famous British Museum.

James ordered High Tea and showed Delia how to spread fresh double clotted cream on the scones and afterwards lather it with raspberry jam.

"This is delicious," Delia said as she sipped her Earl Grey tea from a delicate cup.

When they arrived at the British Museum, Delia was overwhelmed by all the treasures from England and around the world. James guided her through many rooms to the Egyptian and Greco-Roman sections. She sensed his British pride in the cultural wealth gathered on this island in the Atlantic: the beauty of the language inscribed in ancient books, the Viking ships, the Celtic helmets and shields. Delia especially loved the graceful Greek statues of the Nereids, the water nymphs, and the dark mysterious Egyptian tombs of the Pharaohs, painted on the inside with the starry way to follow after death. They got home about eight p.m. that night. Exhausted, they fell into the elegant four poster bed. They were very passionately in love, and they couldn't resist each other. The love between them was immeasurable.

CHAPTER 43

ELIA COULDN'T WAIT TO TELL VICTORIA THE EXCITING NEWS OF HER engagement. She didn't care how much they charged for overseas calls because suddenly she was to be the wealthy wife of James Hicks. She called as soon as James left for the Parliament the next day.

"Hi Vic! I called to tell you my lucky news! The fortune teller told me that I would find my luck in Europe, more specifically England, and it has come true! James begged me to move to London so we would never be away from each other. I asked him if he was asking me to marry him and he said YES! I will only come home to pack my luggage, quit my job, and say goodbye to my friends."

"Oh, Delia, that's wonderful! Every time you call me the news just keeps getting better and better. What are you going to do with the townhouse?" she asked Delia.

"I am going to sell it or rent it but my original plan was just to keep it for a home in D.C. But James wants me to sell it as a first step in giving up my free spirit and becoming totally dependent on him." Delia sighed and Victoria laughed. We are getting married this summer so I still have time to think about it," explained Delia.

"Have you and James planned where you will have the wedding ceremony?" asked Victoria.

"James brought up the idea of getting married on a yacht at the French Riviera or getting married at the beautiful Medieval York Cathedral in his district of Yorkshire where all the dignitaries could attend, or just in the small church by the river that runs through the village where most of his working class constituents live. James owns a Manor house on the hill overlooking the river. We could open our doors for our reception to all the villagers he loves and serves. I'm not quite sure exactly what we are going to do. I think I would fit in better with the common folk rather than the aristocrats," Delia observed.

"Vic, will you be my maid of honor?" Delia excitedly asked. "James will invite Chris to come with you and join us for all the festivities."

Victoria was glad to accept the offer to be part of such a distinguished wedding party and after congratulating each other on finding "Mr. Right", they once again said goodbye.

CHAPTER 44

*I*T WAS ALMOST THE LAST NIGHT BEFORE DELIA WOULD RETURN TO Georgetown to prepare for her new life in England. She thought about the words "last" and "lasting". Delia burst out in tears. She felt that their love affair reminded her of little bubbles. They might break at any time just like every previous love affair she had in the past. She looked down at her engagement ring for security. But this is different than before, she told herself. Scot just quickly married me to get me a visa to stay in the country and Peter never helped me when I became pregnant. But James is courting me like I am royalty. He loves me for my beauty but more than that he loves me for my soul and spirit. He takes time from his busy schedule and important work to teach me about his culture. He genuinely wants me to love his family and friends. He walks and talks with the Lords of Parliament, but he is most at home with the commoners. He is the first man I've met who treats me with respect and dignity. He must be my soulmate. She began to sob from the deep feelings of joy and doubt. James saw her crying and asked her why she was crying as he gently wiped away her tears.

"I just have this strange feeling our relationship is not going to last," she said mournfully. "Why would you say that, Delia?" he asked.

"Because I've had this sort of relationship before and I promised myself not to be involved in it again because I was badly hurt," she said.

"Do you want to talk about it?" he asked.

"No, not now." James respected her wish. They both went to sleep wrapped in the security of their bodies touching each other.

The alarm clock went off at four o'clock in the morning. James had to get up and get ready for work. He told Delia to get some sleep and he would be calling her around ten a.m. He kissed her on the forehead and left for work.

Delia couldn't go back to sleep. She made herself a cup of coffee and sat down on top of the bed. Punctually at ten, James called and said. "I want you to come and meet me here at the House of Commons at four o'clock this afternoon."

She got there a little bit after four o'clock and James already was waiting for her. He kissed her and led her to his car. They rode through the country side until they got to one of James' favorite restaurants called the "Bricks". The inside was made from old English oak wood with high ceiling chandeliers and it overlooked a small blue lake. She was enchanted watching the graceful swans swimming around the gazebo on a small island in the center of the lake. They had several beautiful fireplaces throughout the restaurant. The restaurant was not crowded and the atmosphere had a calming energy. Delia ordered fresh cod and a baked potato with vegetables while James had rib eye steak and baked potato with a salad. The meals were delicious and they drove back to the hotel and shared some herbal tea before they retired for bed. During Delia's last week in London, James tried to spend as much time with her as possible.

The time had come for Delia to return to Washington D.C. She bought a souvenir Buckingham Palace key chain for Victoria and a t-shirt for Chris that said on the front "Victoria Station". Delia's flight was in the evening at six p.m. James drove her to the airport. On the way, they discussed all the practical details concerning Delia's preparation to move to England. When they arrived at Heathrow, they hugged each other and kissed.

It was very emotional for both of them. They knew that they would be together in one month for Christmas break but their wedding date in July seemed a long time away.

"Long distant engagements are so difficult, James. Please don't change your mind while I am gone."

"And don't you sneak off one night to the Zebra Night Club, Delia." They both laughed to release the tension.

"Call me Delia if you need any help in settling matters before you move permanently to be with me forever in England. I have your return ticket tucked in your passport. Don't lose it!" he warned. They said goodbye and Delia was on her way back to Washington D.C.

CHAPTER 45

THE PLANE WAS DELAYED A LITTLE DUE TO AN EARLY WINTER STORM, but Victoria was already waiting for her at the airport to pick her up when she arrived. Delia and Victoria hugged each other. Delia flashed her beautiful engagement ring and Victoria put on her sunglasses, teasing her about the brilliance of the bling.

"I hope I am ready to adapt to the English married woman lifestyle. I really enjoy the freedom I have here" Delia confided to Victoria.

"You know you can have two homes, one here and the second one in England," she told Delia.

"I already thought about that but it would be too much and I don't think James would really like that arrangement."

"Well, what's been happening over here?" Delia asked Victoria on the drive home to Georgetown.

"Chris and I are going to live together. I already moved some of my stuff and I was waiting for you to come back from your trip," Victoria told Delia.

I will help you pack tomorrow," Delia replied.

Victoria moved out of the house three days later and Delia began the process of disentangling herself from life in America.

It was the beginning of December and Delia had finished renting her townhouse and quitting her job and packing her bags and shipping her trunks filled with household items and memorabilia. She was ready for her move to London. Victoria and Delia took one final trip to the mall to buy Christmas presents for every member of James' family. James communicated with her all the time and they spent long hours e-mailing each other every day

James reminded Delia that they were going to spend Christmas with his parents and his sister and brothers in the ancient city of York. Everyone would first come to his house in Yorkshire to meet his future bride. Delia had invited Victoria and Chris to have a "Victorian" Christmas with them in London, but Victoria told her that they were going to visit Chris's parents in Quebec.

CHAPTER 46

ELIA LEFT EARLY FOR LONDON ON DECEMBER 12TH TO AVOID THE Christmas rush at the airport. She boarded her flight and because she was exhausted from moving and packing, she slept like a baby the entire way.

Her flight landed at Heathrow airport at six forty- five on Sunday morning. As usual, the airport was swamped with different people from different flights and from different countries. James and his sister Fiona were already waiting to greet her. She kissed James and he introduced her to Fiona, his sister. She hugged Delia and they went straight to James' car and began their two- and half hour journey to James' manor house in Yorkshire.

Delia thought that the English countryside must have the most beautiful scenery in the world. Even though it was winter, it was still charming. Delia and Fiona talked about the history of England on the way. Fiona explained how they thatched the roofs of many cottages in the quaint villages. She told her they named Oxford after the place in the river where the oxen could ford the stream and she pointed out where Shakespeare lived in Stratford on the Avon River. She seemed to know the story behind every castle too and she graciously shared all this knowledge with Delia on their journey home. Finally, James announced they were about ten minutes away from his house which was named Manor Heights. Delia smiled with relief. The ivy-covered manor house sat up on the top of the hill overlooking the beautiful meadow and farms. Green hedge rows and holly trees and exquisite rose gardens and terraces with fountains surrounded the home. Delia had to pinch herself to realize that all this would soon be her home too. James took all the bags and suitcases inside the house. It had an upstairs with five bedrooms. There were two grand bedrooms downstairs. It had four and half bathrooms and four fireplaces.

It was damp and freezing cold outside, so James lit the fireplace right away as his sister Fiona began to prepare the dinner. James told Delia that she would be sleeping in his room, the grand bedroom fireplace suite, while he would sleep in one of the guest bedrooms upstairs. James' room had a picture window with clear lead glass where Delia could see the view of the English meadows. The trees still were bedecked with some late autumn leaves and the cows and sheep were grazing on the heath. She stepped through the bedroom's sliding glass door onto an Italian style terrace with ivy covered trellises. She marveled at a carved lion's head perched at the top of a fountain, roaring water from its regal mouth down three tiers to an embellished basin below. Delia felt centuries of history and nobility in James' home. In a way, she felt in her heart, that James was like his home, welcoming to both shepherds and kings.

James told Delia that Fiona was a barrister in London and had to go back to work the next day. She had been helping James and his servants clean the house most of the weekend. He had been staying there infrequently since the summertime. The phone rang and it was his father.

"Has Delia arrived safely," he asked.

"Yes, Dad, she arrived early this morning and I went with Fiona to pick her up from Heathrow," James told his father.

"I'm glad she has arrived and we'll see you this weekend," said his father.

"You're very lucky," said James.

"Why is that?" Delia asked James.

"You are going to meet my entire family this weekend. We have to buy more food and drinks, Delia! They eat a lot of food! "James said laughing at the same time.

Fiona quickly defended her family. "Delia don't listen to my brother! He's being cheeky,"

Fiona pinched her brother on his cheek and laughed really loud. Delia felt comfortable and at home. They all sat down around a smaller Victorian table by the fireplace in the kitchen and broke bread together.

Fiona made roasted leg of lamb, mashed potatoes, gravy, chestnut stuffing, green beans, and apple sauce. The dinner was very delicious and dessert was a special English truffle cake with rum. A light snow began to fall and sparkle outside the window. They sat around the fireplace and drank some English tea, ate cake, and shared stories. It was the most romantic moment that Delia had ever experienced in her life. Delia's engagement ring also sparkled in the light of the fire. James kissed Delia goodnight and left the two future sisters to chat in the dwindling firelight. Fiona opened a bottle of special Christmas brandy and poured two elegant crystal glasses to the brim.

"I'm glad you met my brother. You're smart and beautiful," said Fiona. "I remember when he first went to Washington D.C. After he got home, he called me up and told me that he met someone that he really liked. I met her at this African club, he told me.

"That doesn't sound very good, meeting someone in a night club," I told my brother. "That's a pick up place and you're just wasting your time," Fiona said.

Fiona recounted that James told her that he wasn't wasting his time and he thought he had met the love of his life, someone who was going to love him forever.

"So many times, Delia, my brother kept telling me that someday he was going to see you again and sure enough, he was right, and I have never seen him so happy. He told me about your visit last month. He didn't want you to go back to Washington D.C. because he was afraid, he might lose you. I told him to take it slowly but now that I've met you, I understand why he even went faster to secure your hand in marriage."

"It certainly has been a whirlwind romance," Delia replied.

"As you have seen, my brother has a very hectic life. You know being a politician is not easy but I'm very proud of my brother. I have two other brothers and they are both going to be here this weekend and they are both barristers in London who are "lawyers" like me," explained Fiona to Delia.

"Wow! What a very smart family!" said Delia.

"You won't believe this, but my dad is also an attorney," said Fiona. "We seem to have a monopoly on the law!"

"What does your mother do?" Delia asked.

"My mother is a school teacher and I know you're going to love our mother. She likes cooking, gardening and shopping," Fiona said.

"We will have a lot in common," Delia replied.

"I have never seen my brother so happy as tonight and I can see how he loves you, Delia, said Fiona with deep admiration and maybe a wee bit too much brandy.

"I love your brother deeply too. I told him I knew we were soulmates when we first locked eyes!"

"James just told me that you are going to spend Christmas with us here and New Years with our cousins on the French Riviera," said Fiona with flushed cheeks.

"Yes, I just know we are going to have a wonderful time together," Delia said sleepily. And now if you will excuse me, dear Fiona, I fear it is past my bedtime. I look forward to our time together this magical Christmas."

Delia was very tired and she had jet lag and she couldn't wait to go to bed. She hugged her soon to be sister-in-law and thanked her for her hospitality and loving conversation and bid her "Goodnight."

CHAPTER 47

THE NEXT DAY WAS MONDAY AND FIONA HAD TO GO BACK TO WORK IN London. James and Delia gave her a ride back to London. It took two hours to get to London. They went and had some breakfast before they dropped her off at her office. Then they did some grocery shopping and headed back home again. James left again for work in London late that afternoon. Delia was home alone because James had an emergency session in Parliament. He was exhausted from driving back and forth all day so he told Delia he would be staying at the hotel. "Make yourself at home darling and I will be back in your arms as soon as possible," he lamented.

Delia spent the night alone but she got up very early in the morning and made some banana pancakes and some tea. James arrived at seven o'clock in the evening and they were very happy to be alone together again.

James needed to return to London the next day to attend his last session of Parliament before the Christmas break. Delia accompanied him and she went and waited for him at the hotel where they usually stayed. Delia occupied her time by shopping at the boutiques around the hotel. She bought two dresses with pink floral prints and a pair of red shoes. She found out quickly that London was more expensive than Washington D.C. and that English pounds were not equal to American dollars.

However, she remembered that soon she would be the wealthy wife of the famous James Hicks, so she decided to go to Harrods, the world's most famous department store, to do a bit more Christmas shopping. She stood in a queue outside the hotel to jump on a double decker red bus. She climbed the narrow winding steps to the top deck in the open air. She felt especially festive, enjoying all the Christmas decorations on the streets and in the shop windows while she bundled her coat tighter around her lithe body. She arrived at Harrods and found a table where she could sit down and relax and even buy some macaroons to tithe her appetite until dinner with James. She bought herself a blue sweater that was perfect to wear during walks in the cold crisp air in Yorkshire. When she stepped outside to wait for her bus, she bought some roasted chestnuts from a street vendor on the corner who wrapped them in a cone of old newspaper and wished her Merry Christmas with his chipper Cockney accent. She felt like she was falling in love with Merry Ole England as her new home.

She decided with all the Christmas traffic in Knightsbridge, she would forgo the bus and instead travel by way of the underground. She walked to the tube station and enjoyed the talented musicians busking in the underground maze of halls. Around one corner, a quartet was singing in perfect harmony, "We Wish you a Merry Christmas" and around the next corner, a busker sat alone and played on her sliver flute "Hark the Herald Angels Sing". Delia stopped and put a pound tip in each cup as she passed. Leaving the cacophony of sound behind her, Delia stepped into the packed train and headed back to the hotel. James came and picked her up and they were on their way back to Manor Heights. After they had their dinner, Delia wanted to go to bed because she was still very tired from all of her new adventures.

The next day, Friday, James took Delia to do some more grocery shopping to get ready for Christmas and his family's visit. They drove to the village and bought fruits from his favorite vendor at the market, including, apples, oranges, bananas, pears and tangerines as well as a Christmas fruitcake. They also bought winter vegetables: turnips, Brussel sprouts, red beets, cauliflower and leeks. Their final stop was the local butcher, the best in Yorkshire, who provided them with a side of beef and two legs of lamb.

When they returned home, the butler carried in the groceries and the cook began preparing dishes for the upcoming dinners. Delia helped James to put up the vintage Victorian Christmas decorations all around the grand room where they hung fresh evergreen boughs and red holly from the sturdy wooden beams. In the center of this grand 19th century room was the crowning glory, a fourteen-foot Noble pine tree the butler had cut down from their property. The maid was busy putting real beeswax candles in crystal holders on every branch. A beautiful 17th century Italian creche James inherited from his grandmother was placed under the tree. His parents were going to spend three days with them and his two brothers and his sister were going to be with the newly engaged couple until Sunday. James told Delia that his sister really enjoyed her company and he knew the whole family were going to like her too.

CHAPTER 48

*E*VERYONE ARRIVED IN THE AFTERNOON AND HIS PARENTS, STEVE AND Joanna arrived first. James went and helped them with their bags and brought them to the house. He introduced Delia to his parents as they entered the door.

"We have heard so much about you, Delia," said James's mother to Delia.

"I'm glad to meet both of you," responded Delia.

"How was the weather in Washington D.C. when you left?" asked Steve.

"It's very cold there right now and a storm just left six inches of fresh snow. It made it almost impossible to drive on the Belt way. People just don't know how to drive in the stormy weather. But thankfully I made it to the airport just in time for my flight," replied Delia.

"England can be very damp and the cold can just sink into your bones, if you are not careful, "Joanna said. Be sure to bundle up when you and James enjoy your country walks together."

"Come, let's gather by the fire and drink some mulled wine while we wait for the others to arrive," James suggested.

"Oh James, how thoughtful of you. You remembered how I love the smell of cinnamon and nutmeg and other spices steaming from my hot wine glass," Joanna said with motherly pride.

The rest of James's relatives arrived at six o'clock in the evening. They all greeted Delia and it was time to have a traditional Advent Sunday dinner of roast beef and Yorkshire pudding with gravy. Everyone sat around the table and enjoyed their dinner and the beautiful Advent decorations. His brothers started talking about the news in London and the world. Because James worked in the Parliament, most of the family couldn't wait to ask him about the latest debates between party members and of course the latest gossip about the English royalty.

Afterwards, they all sat around the fireplace sipping brandy and eating fruit cake, sharing the news of the Hicks family members. They were all looking forward to celebrating Christmas next Sunday at their parent's stately family home in York. Delia excused herself saying that she needed to retire to her bed because she was still on Chicago time. Everyone said good night to her and James told her lovingly that a good brisk walk in the English countryside would be a boon to her soul and health in the morning. Everyone retired for bed about midnight. James couldn't go to sleep right away. He was thinking about Delia. He went to her room and peered at her but she was deep asleep. He went back up to his guest room and finally drifted away in pleasant dreams of the future with Delia.

CHAPTER 49

DELIA GOT UP VERY EARLY IN THE MORNING AND WENT OUTSIDE TO breathe some fresh air. She looked at the meadows and saw all these beautiful wild birds fly across the clear blue sky and she saw sheep and cows in the farm close by. It was a beautiful view from James's house. She could see the river over yonder and she went back to the house and changed her clothes to some warmer ones. She wore the red sweater which James had given her last month and her blue winter coat, gloves, boots and her very special Irish woven white wool hat and scarf. She decided to take a walk down the trail below the house. She saw some people walking down there near a big red barn. She started feeling better as she walked down the trail. As she got closer to the barn, she met the owner. They greeted each other and she complimented them on how well kept the barn was and how sweet their wooly sheep were. They invited her in the house and asked her if she wanted to have some tea.

"I am staying up in that house on the hill," she told them. "By the way, my name is Delia," she added smiling.

"This is Tommy, my husband, and my name is Patricia Lord and we are both happy to meet you," she said.

"You know James Hicks, the great politician?" Tommy asked incredulously.

"Yes" Delia replied. "The whole family is here for Christmas."

"Very good family and they are quiet well known here," said Patricia. "Mr. Hicks represents us well in Parliament. He is always arguing on behalf of the local farmers."

"Well, I really must go now," Delia said. "That was a very nice tea Mr. and Mrs. Lord, thank you very much," she told them.

"Do you like fruitcake?" asked Tommy. "Please take this cake back with you for the Hicks family to enjoy. It is my wife's special Christmas recipe," said Tommy proudly.

"I just love fruitcake and thank you very much," Delia said while heading for the door. "I better run before they start looking for me," she said.

"Please come again," said Patricia.

"I will", she said. "I'll tell James all about our special visit!" Delia told Tommy.

Everyone was up and James was looking for Delia. "There you are! Where did you disappear to?" asked James.

"I took a walk down to the barn, and guess who I met?" Delia said a little out of breath from her vigorous climb back up the hill.

"Who?" asked James.

"The Lords, the farmers at the foot of the hill." Delia excitedly told James.

"They are kind people," said James warmly smiling at his rosy cheeked bride to be.

"They gave me some peaches and pears, and they invited me to have some tea with them at their house," she told James

"Delia, everyone around here knows them and they very kind people. They know my family very well, too," James said.

"Yes, that's what they told me. I better watch out that I don't do anything bad," said Delia laughing.

His mother was fixing a hearty English breakfast when she called out to Delia, "Are you feeling better dear?"

"Much better Joanna, and thank you for asking," Delia replied.

"So, you went down to the barn?" she asked Delia.

"It's really beautiful down there, and I love to see the cows and sheep grazing together in the meadow," she told Joanna. "I want to go down to the river. The Lords told me they have stores and restaurants down there," she said.

"The river is beautiful in the springtime and summer," said Joanna. "That's when people come down here and take a ride in the boat down the river. You and James will be able to visit in the spring or summer as you plan your wedding and ride in one of these Holiday boats," she said.

James's two brothers, Eric and Ian, all left the next day to go back to work in London while James's parents stayed with Delia and James for the next three days. Delia was very excited to meet James's parents and she was glad that they spent more time together. James father, Steve, told Delia that he and Joanna had visited Washington D.C and New York as well.

"Most Americans do not realize that New York was named after our home city, the old York." Joanna said with a twinkle in her eyes.

With Joanna's understated British sense of humor, Delia began to realize that she often couldn't tell the difference between a criticism or a compliment. Although they all spoke the same language around the dinner table, there were so many different nuances and accents and even different words for the same thing, she often felt foolish and confused. Steve told her last night that her jumper was in the boot of the car and she had no idea that he was talking about her sweater in the trunk. Ian asked her if she was going to let her townhouse in Georgetown and she had responded, "Let my townhouse do what?" They all laughed and said they meant if she was going to rent. Sometimes she felt they were laughing *at* her and not *with* her when they imitated her American accent, but James said to just let it all roll off her back like a duck in the water.

During breakfast, Joanna pointed out to Delia that Yorkshire was where the working class lived so she should feel right at home.

"We have a lot of coal mines and farms in this region, and most of the workers belong to the Labor Party, which James represents," she explained to Delia.

"You're very lucky to have such a great family. All your children are all well-educated and hold very exciting professions. I met your daughter, Fiona, last week and she is beautiful and smart," Delia told Joanna.

"Three of my children are all attorneys, and one as you know, is a great politician, whom I'm very proud of. He always talks about you, Delia, and you're very special to him. He told us that you came and spent ten days with him last month and that is when he knew for sure that you were the woman God made for him," James' mother said as an affirming sign of acceptance to Delia.

"Yes, Delia said with a sweet smile, "the trip last month was the turning point in our relationship. James asked me to marry him and bought me this beautiful ring as a symbol of his commitment to be married this summer."

"Well, it has been a rather rushed affair, but I'm so glad that you are here to spend the Holidays with us," Joanna told Delia.

James parents left on Thursday to go back to York, and they said again how much they were looking forward to spending more time with Delia and James for Christmas.

CHAPTER 50

THE SERVANTS HELPED JAMES TIDY THE HOUSE WHILE DELIA STARTED packing their bags again to go to the city of York. It would be about an hour drive to reach his parents' house. When they woke up early Saturday morning, it was bright and sunny. They looked out of the bedroom window and saw the sun shining on a light frost covering the trees, the grounds and the roads like a comforter of sparkling diamonds. They both hoped the slippery driving conditions would not cause them to be late for the Christmas Eve service. The entire family planned on attending the Anglican Mass at the majestic 12th century York cathedral. James told Delia that all of England considered this national treasure to be one of the finest examples of Christian Medieval architecture and stain glass artistry in the world.

The countryside was peaceful and each quaint village they passed through was decorated with little pine trees posted above the market doors as an anchor for the colored lights arching across to the other side, like a bridge of joy and hope. Many villagers were out and about buying last minute gifts and food for their family feast. Smoke curled like ribbons above the thatched roofs. Delia loved the natural simplicity and festive mood.

After a half hour of driving, James asked Delia if she could drive because he was a little tired. The English people drive on the left side of the road with the steering wheel on the right, the exact opposite of how Delia had learned to drive in America. She again pondered that two cultures who spoke the same language could actually be so different.

She started off slowly, until she got used to the car and the road. She tried to stay focused with her eyes on the road so she wouldn't be distracted by all of the lovely sights. They drove up a steep hill and Delia thought she was going to lose control of the car, but she kept a steady speed until they reached the very top and James asked her to stop the car. They both got out from the car and stretched their legs and arms. "Come here, Delia! I want to show you something," and he pointed down the hill." Look down there! That's Yorkshire in her finest array," he told Delia.

"God, it's so beautiful" she yelled into the frigid wind. They went back to the car and Delia started driving downhill slowly.

The hill was really steep and winding and she could see the North Sea in the distance with sheep and cows grazing down to the cliffs. She had to be careful not to wander with her eyes too much in order to avoid a catastrophic crash. She noticed the homes were large but built differently from the ones in the United States. As soon as they reached the bottom of the hill, James told her to make a right turn on Brown Street and keep going straight until they came to Cliff Street and then make a quick left turn, until they reached Willow Drive. I want you to keep going until you see the house on the righthand side. It is a large white brick house and the address is 1457 Willow Drive. Delia found the house right away and she parked in the elegant circular drive with a majestic fountain at the front entrance to his parents' home.

"You did very well, Delia, for a foreigner" James said laughing.

"That was a scary ride for me as the driver. I thought I was going to roll the car downhill," she told James as he gave her hug of encouragement.

His parents were very happy to see them again. James told them that Delia drove most of the way to the house.

"What a brave young lady," James' father said to Delia, holding his hand out politely to escort her into their home. "Now come in and join the rest of the family for a cup of spiked eggnog to take the chill off your bones," James' father jovially commanded.

It was Christmas Eve and the outer light had dimmed, but the fireplace hearth where the family had gathered was lit by a roaring Yule Log. Fiona was very happy to see Delia again. Eric and Ian formally greeted Delia and heartily embraced their brother, James.

"I heard that you drove all the way here," Fiona told Delia.

"Oh yes, it was a rough one," said Delia laughing." I barely had time to enjoy the beautiful Yorkshire scenery."

The family home was spacious and comfortable. It had an upstairs with five bedrooms and four and half baths.

"All our children grew up in this house," Joanna proudly told Delia, "and here are their pictures when they were really small."

"Look at James," Delia commented." He was the cutest one of all!"

After a special Christmas Eve feast of farm fresh turkey with chestnut dressing, everyone sat around the fireplace, talking about politics and plans for the upcoming 12 days of Christmas festivities. When they heard "The First Noel" ring out from the tall bell towers of York Cathedral, they extinguished the candles on the Victorian Christmas tree with a solid silver snuffer and said a prayer for peace. As they walked several blocks to attend midnight mass, Delia marveled at the silver stars shining so brightly in the black velvet sky.

Christmas day was wonderful and everyone exchanged gifts. They were thankful for Delia bringing all their presents from Washington D.C. She gave everyone a sweater embellished with a picture of the Capitol Building, the American equivalent to the English Parliament. She brought for James a beautiful oil painting of Washington D.C. "I thank you, dearest Delia, for the painting, but your presence in my life is the greatest gift of all," James said with a sincere smile. They all admired her gifts and thanked Delia for her thoughtfulness.

James's parents gave her a beautiful yellow sweater, a scarf, and a pair of matching gloves. James' two brothers gave her a journal where they sarcastically joked, "she could keep all her notes about English politics." Fiona gave her a pair of black leather boots and James gave her a gift card from Harrods for five hundred English pounds. Delia was very happy and surprised that James' family had welcomed her so royally.

After their gift exchange, they sat around the table and had their Christmas dinner that Joanna had prepared: a leg of lamb, potatoes, and vegetables. Delia was surprised to see festive Christmas "crackers", bright tubes covered with silver foil, at each place setting. As they enjoyed a dessert of fruit and crème truffle, they pulled the string and popped their "cracker". Bright colored streamers and funny presents fell out onto the table. Everyone put on paper hats and laughed and drank hot buttered rum. The family enjoyed this special day, especially the joy of having Delia as a guest of honor.

"The New Year's highlight will be your wedding in July," Fiona said and the whole family began to sing a local wassailing song as they passed a cup of spiced wine one last time.

CHAPTER *51*

THE FOLLOWING DAY, JAMES AND DELIA HAD TO RETURN TO LONDON to prepare for their New Year's trip to Paris and the French Riviera. They said goodbye to the family and off they went on their journey back to London. They were both tired when they arrived at the hotel. James' friends and cousins in France had already left him messages about their plans for the New Year's Eve party. They rose early the next morning to catch their flight to Paris.

When they arrived, Delia understood why they call Paris a city for lovers. She loved all the gold embellished bridges over the romantic river Seine and the tall elegant windows of the French architecture. Luckily, James was fluent in French so the local Parisians respected them when they asked for directions.

After touring Notre Dame Cathedral, James took her on a tourist bateau ride down the river Seine to hear the history of Paris. After a light lunch of crepes in a corner café, she and James strolled the Champs-Elysees. James bought her exquisite jewelry and high fashioned silk dresses for her to wear to all the parties they would attend in the south of France on the French Rivera. After a fine French dining experience in their hotel, they enjoyed a couple's massage before retiring to their tall canopied bed. The canopy covering like the window draperies were sewn from silk brocade woven in rich burgundy and gold threads. A fine medieval silk tapestry of a Lady and a unicorn hung on the wall. Delia felt that she was that lucky lady that the fortuneteller, Maria, had predicted.

In the morning, after a breakfast of butter croissants and expresso, they hailed a taxi for the Gard du Sud. They boarded their private compartment on the train that traveled through the castle and wine country of the Loire Valley south to the French Rivera.

"We have to get dressed now, Delia," James said after they checked into their hotel. We need to meet my cousins tonight. They both took a quick shower and got dressed. Delia wore the short black silk dress that James bought for her in Paris. She accessorized it with a string of pearls and diamonds with matching earrings. She brushed her long black hair up into a French twist and stepped into her black high heeled shoes. James wore a dark blue suit and a light blue shirt. The color of his clothing highlighted his Mediterranean blue eyes.

James admired Delia's simple elegance when she emerged from the changing room. "You look fabulous tonight, Delia! I'm glad that I bought you the dress and jewelry in Paris. Every duchess at the party will envy your beauty," he said in his teasing tone of voice. Delia had expressed to him more than once her lack of confidence in mingling with the rich and famous. She thanked James with a kiss, trying not to get her lipstick mark on his cheek.

They drove down to the restaurant where they were going to meet James's four cousins. The evening was cool and people were walking about the village and listening to the romantic French music pouring out of every beach front café. James introduced Delia to his four cousins and they were all extremely wealthy good-looking individuals. They all welcomed Delia to the French Riviera. The atmosphere in the restaurant was warm and the patrons very rich. The women all wore expensive designer gold jewelry and expensive French perfume permeated the atmosphere.

Everyone was polite which included the waiters and waitresses. The restaurant was very French and no one spoke a single word of English. Delia felt bad because everyone around her spoke fluent French and she couldn't even read the menu. James embodied chivalry. He spoke perfect French and always covered for Delia, protecting her from social embarrassment. If someone engaged her in a conversation, she just graciously nodded her beautiful head in agreement. Every once and a while, she would accentuate her head nodding with her one French word 'oui' in French accent. By the end of the dinner of broiled lobster, pommes

Terre au gratin and fine French wine, everyone felt Delia was quiet but an excellent listener!

After dinner they all went to the yacht and watched the glittering lights of the French Riviera from different hotels, buildings and homes. The ocean was calm while the waves slowly rocked the boats. The beautiful full silver moon reflected in the ocean with the twinkling stars. Delia thought the Riviera to be the most romantic place on earth and James, a gallant knight in shiny armor who rescued his lovely lady!

CHAPTER *52*

*T*HEY WENT BACK TO THE HOTEL, OPENED THE WINDOWS TO LET THE cool ocean breezes float through, and wrapped in each other's arms, they slept peacefully through the night.

The next morning, the last day of the year, December 31, Delia called Victoria in D.C. Delia asked her about Chris. "Everything is going well, between the two of us," she said. "I have some good news to tell you," she said.

"What is it?" asked Delia.

"I'm pregnant," Victoria proudly announced.

"Congratulations! I'm so happy for you, Vic. You will have quite a bump showing at my wedding in July!" Delia said kidding her. Are you and Chris going to get married?"

"No, I don't think so," Victoria said disappointedly. Quickly changing the subject, Victoria asked "How was your trip and your Christmas?"

"Oh Vic, I had a very wonderful time. I met all his family and they are all very smart and fun to be with. I am going to enjoy being part of this family. His sister Fiona, and his two brothers are all attorneys, including their father. Their mother, Joanna, is a school teacher. We all went to York and spent Christmas there in the home where James grew up. We flew to Paris as soon as we returned to London. Tonight, on New Year's Eve, James and I will attend one of James's friend's party with his four very wealthy cousins and their wives. And you know Vic, it is a tradition to predict the future on New Year's Eve. And guess what? Maria, the medium was right: I am one lucky girl and you are pregnant with your first child!"

New Year's Eve was marked by champagne and hors d'oeuvres on his cousin's yacht overlooking the ocean at Saint Tropez. Hundreds of people were gathered on the docks to look at the decorated yachts and of course the fireworks show at midnight.

Delia felt giddy when they left the party on the yacht and the many trendy bars to return to their private villa. James, flushed with champagne and manly desire, carried Delia onto their private beach and into their private grass hut. Delia was dreaming of her home in the Savu Island as they made passionate love.

CHAPTER 53

*I*T WAS A COLD WEEK IN EARLY MARCH WHEN DELIA TOOK A BREAK FROM making wedding plans. She had been nauseated almost every morning for the past month. She sometimes stayed alone in Yorkshire at Manor Heights when James was at work, but this week she accompanied him to London. Today she had an appointment with his doctor. He was tired after a day battling for new coal safety laws in Parliament, but she was eager to have a conversation about a tabloid she had read at breakfast. She really didn't know much about James' past romances and she was irritated after hearing about it in this sordid way.

Delia perched rigidly on the velvet red couch, waiting for James to return from Parliament. As soon as he entered the front door, Delia called out for him to join her in the sitting room of their hotel suite.

"James, I read a disturbing article about you and a woman from your past in the Mirror today. Please tell me about Clara Sinclair, this *super model* that you were once going to marry."

James was exhausted from debating thorny issues on the floor of Parliament all day, but he could see that Delia was confused and upset, so he calmly agreed to tell her all.

"She was beautiful and the most sexually potent woman that I've known, but I realized we would be disastrous together in the long run. We would end up fighting each other," James finished with a small grin.

He sat back in the sofa, his eyes on Delia and she was silent for a while, digesting his words, and then she said slowly, "Because you were so volatile together is that what you mean?" asked Delia.

"Exactly, we never had a quiet moment," said James.

"You were not compatible?" Delia asked.

"Not in any way except in bed, but one cannot build a lasting relationship on sex alone," said James.

Delia nodded and eyed him carefully, then confided. "I've always heard people say that compatibility between a man and a woman was the most important thing of all. And I know you and I are compatible."

"Clara was a wonderful woman when I knew her, but she was not right for me, nor I for her, not on a normal everyday level. We were far too explosive, and it was my fault as much as hers. Obviously, there was a great deal of empathy there," said James. "I was also in love with her. It just wasn't enough for a steady stable life," he said smiling at Delia.

Then, Delia smiled back at him. The two of them were seated on the loveseat in their spacious hotel suite in London. A framed portrait of Queen Victoria hung on the wall behind the couch, behind the politician and the young island girl. Two people who had only just discovered each other's existence, and wanted to understand each other, and to find closeness, and to be lovers forever. The younger striving to comprehend a disastrous long-ago relationship, the older politician hoping that this past action would not damage him too badly in her eyes in the present.

CHAPTER 54

THEY RETURNED TO MANOR HEIGHTS FOR THE WEEKEND. DELIA HAD just confided over breakfast that she had been to see Sir Harvey, his private doctor, while she was in London. She was waiting for the results. James seemed to be in shock and said nothing as he pondered the implications of such a report.

The silence was broken by the ringing of the telephone, starling them both. It almost instantly stopped; the phone had been answered elsewhere in the house by a staff member. A moment later the maid appeared at the doorway. "Excuse me, sir, Sir Harvey is on the phone and he would like to talk to you," said the maid. "Thank you, Jane" responded James. James took the call in his study and excused himself from Delia. "Good morning Jack?" said James.

Delia rose and walked across to the French doors which opened on to the terrace of the ancient manor house. She went outside, closing the door behind. She took several deep breaths. The air was always so clean and fresh up in the dales. It was a beautiful morning in early March. The sky was azure blue with white puffy clouds and hints of Spring. A sunny golden day filled with pristine light, as it had been yesterday and the day before. She had grown to love this crystalline light, which she had discovered was so prevalent in the north of England.

She sat down on the stone bench and stared across the wide green lawns that splayed out from the house. She admired the stately rose garden. She contemplated her dilemma. She worried that she had rushed into committing to marry James before considering all the possible obstacles to her happiness. She told herself it was like when she married Scott when she was too young and naïve.

She analyzed herself and thought: "I know I am definitely a romantic, artistic and spontaneous. I passionately jump into relationships, like with Peter, without thinking about the consequences. I think the problem with me is that I am too independent, and a free spirit needs to stay free."

She remembered what Victoria told her when she was uncertain about marrying James: "But when luck knocks on your door you better grab it, Delia. You can't be single the rest of your life. We need to share our lives with someone who really loves us and you don't want to be miserable all the time and always worrying about meeting someone new. That sort of life style is getting old and you need to move on," Victoria said in her no-nonsense voice, now playing like a tape recorder from the past in Delia's mind.

But today she was confused again. She could hear Victoria's voice in her head again telling her to "stop thinking so much; just enjoy your life together." But she knew her life with James would always be open, like a microscope, to public scrutiny and she did not know if she could stand the lack of freedom she would feel always being in the public eye…and they could say anything they wanted in their gossipy news…like about Clara and James. She also knew that James was loving but set in his ways. She sensed it would be difficult for him to adjust to her spontaneous ways. She feared that James, who was so used to living by himself would suddenly realize he had to share his wealth with someone so poor and common for the rest of his life. She convinced herself that he would leave her when the passion faded into boredom with her. …and if I am pregnant, we are both trapped. She broke down crying.

At that precise moment, James came to the terrace, interrupting her self-pitying reverie.

"Oh, there you are darling. I've been looking everywhere for you…to share *our* good news!" When he noticed her tears, he said "I hope these are tears of joy for you have made me the happiest husband and father to be in the world!

"I'm really in love with you, James and there's no one else for me but you. It just this thing about your politician status that really scares me," she confessed. And now that I am pregnant before our wedding, the reporters will circle us like sharks smelling blood in the water.

"Delia, everything is going to be okay. I will protect you and I understand what you're thinking. I promise you that everything will be fine. Please Delia, don't worry about anything."

"All right, I will still marry you, James, even though I *have* to now for the sake of our baby" she said embracing him with sudden joy.

"Oh! my darling, you have just made me a very happy politician," James said. They both broke out laughing.

"This is the happiest day of our lives and I know we've made the right choice... and God, as a sign of His heavenly approval, has blessed us with a baby to boot!" James said lifting Delia's spirit. "But shush, let's not tell anyone our secret except our families and best friends!"

CHAPTER 55

"*L*ET'S CALL MY PARENTS NOW AND TELL THEM THE GOOD NEWS," HE TOLD Delia. His parents were very happy to learn that they were now grandparents in waiting! They also called Fiona and his two brothers and they accepted this delicate situation and were very happy about the news. Fiona wanted to speak to Delia.

"Congratulations, Delia! I'm so happy that you are going to marry my brother and have his baby. I am so excited to be your baby's aunt. You will be very proud marrying him. He is a wonderful and loving man."

"I know, I really love your brother very much," she said.

"Well Delia, now you're going to be together forever" said Fiona.

"I don't know if that's going to be a good idea!"

"I just love your sense of humor, Delia," laughed Fiona.

"Have you ever wondered sometimes Fiona why we marry certain men?"

"I believe we are destined to meet this man or marry him and no one can really change that, even if we handle the love in a right or wrong way. But we cannot really change the law of the universe, and we can't really ask why things have to happen this way. One thing I know for sure, we have a special voice deep inside us, telling us this is the right man for us. This is why we should listen to our inner self. My deepest inner feeling was telling me that James is the right man for me to marry."

"Well Delia, that's very good philosophical advice. I will remember to listen more deeply when I meet my next bloke in a pub!" she said breaking the serious mood.

You know Fiona, all kidding aside, "my gracious mother called me last year and she asked me about James."

"Delia, I hope this man is going to work for you this time. How did you meet this man?" my mother asked.

"I met him at this night club in Washington D.C.," Delia told her mother. "Oh no, Delia, I don't like the sound of it," said my mother.

"Really? that was my response too about you," Fiona admitted laughing.

"It is okay mother, I said, this man is a well- known politician and I've read his name in the news and he's done a lot of good things for his country."

"Why don't you find someone who is working class, Delia? I feel this man is too high class and wealthy for you," my mother said.

"Mother, listen to me," I told her lovingly. "He is a gentleman and he cares for the working class like you and me. Our meeting was divinely ordained and would have always been, whether we met in a church or a pub!"

"I hope you meet my mother someday, Fiona. She is funny, intelligent and always worrying about everything.

"I look forward to that Fiona replied, especially now that we are all one family."

CHAPTER 56

THE MONTH OF APRIL SEEMED TO FLY BY LIKE THE BIRDS OUTSIDE IN THE trellises busy building their nests. Many wedding plans were revised to accommodate the fact of Delia's pregnancy. The little church in the village by the river was chosen as the perfect location. After the wedding, the guests would be invited to a small but lavish reception at Manor Heights. The wedding list was cut from eight hundred guests to just fifty of their closest friends and family. The date was moved to June 1st which happened to be Whitsun or Pentecost in America, 50 days after Easter. Known as the birthday of the church, everyone in England wears white to church that Sunday. Delia thought it was a special touch that she would not be the only one wearing white.

Delia hired a special designer and gifted seamstress to sew both Victoria's dress and her wedding dress to conceal their pregnancies at six months. But they could not conceal their joy that they both would have little boys to become best friends like their mothers.

The month of May always arrives in England with the promise of flowers to brighten the grey landscape. Under a clear blue sky, Delia rose on May 1st early and walked down the trail to see the Lords.

The meadows and the hills were beautiful light green and the cows and the sheep were grazing in the field. Patricia Lord greeted Delia near the barn and said, "How wonderful to see you again! Let's go inside the house."

Her husband, Tommy, was still out in the field feeding all the cows and sheep. They sat down and had some tea and English scones. Patricia's husband appeared at the door and he greeted her with a big smile.

"I'm happy to see you again, Delia," he said. "The month of May is a wonderful time to come and visit this part of the country. Tell the politician to take you to the river," he said.

"I will go straight away and tell him," she replied.

Delia gave them a box of chocolates she bought for them while in Paris and Patricia gave her some fruits and bread which she had just baked that morning. They were very thankful and Delia told them that she was going to ask James to take her to the river that afternoon.

James was already up when she got home. "I went to the Lords and gave them a box of Parisian chocolates," said Delia.

"That was very nice of you," he said. "We'll be going down to the river this afternoon to see what's happening during the village May Day celebrations. This is the time of the year when everyone gathers at the river. You know, if we are lucky, we can see the village children dancing around the maypole with colored ribbons," he said.

They prepared themselves to go down to the river.

"Are you going to be all right today, Delia?" asked James.

"Yes of course," she replied.

"You'll love the river. There are many different kinds of restaurants and stores around the bank of the river," James said. "There is always a large crowd of people not only the locals but also from all over the world." They decided not to drive but walked instead and the fresh air was good for both of them.

James went to meet the Lords and then they continued their walk down to the river. As they got closer to the river, they saw all kinds of people and hundreds of cars were parked nearby. The river was beautiful. They saw many people on the barges and boats going down the river. James met some friends and told them to come up to the house that night for a drink. They walked all over the town and saw many boutiques and tourist shops. They had been walking for three hours before they decided to have a late lunch at a local pub called the "River Tavern."

James explained to Delia the history of the river in this village. He told her that during the eighteenth century, before they had paved roads, the river was one of the ways people would travel from town to town. This village was their meeting place. Some of the quaint shops have been here for centuries. After lunch, they listened to Celtic musicians playing folk songs on their fiddles and making rhythm with spoons in the town square. Young girls with ribbons in their hair danced to some Scottish tunes. Delia, feeling heavy with her pregnancy, enjoyed watching their feet lightly leap to the rhythm with their arms held gracefully poised above, much like ballet dancers.

Their boat ride was beautiful and the English country side was just barely beginning to bloom. There were about 50 passengers on board, mostly tourists. Even though, it was the first day of May, the temperature was still chilly. People were enjoying the sunshine, but Delia pulled her shawl tighter around her shoulder. They both enjoyed their boat trip and they returned home to Manor Heights about six o'clock in the evening.

CHAPTER 57

*J*UNE IST WAS APPROACHING. VICTORIA, AND CHRIS BOOKED THEIR FLIGHTS to go to England for the wedding. They left a few days early because Victoria had to makes sure her Maid of Honor dress would not show her baby bump. James best friend from his days at Oxford flew in to be the best man.

The big day finally arrived and the little village church was packed with James' friends and relatives. Everyone was wearing white to celebrate Whitsun and to celebrate the marriage of their favorite politician and his island bride.

James' family welcomed their guests at the door and James' brothers led them to their pew. Fiona joined Victoria to be a bridesmaid for Delia. They both wore light blue silk chiffon dresses with empire waists to match Delia's style and carried bouquets made of royal blue irises and simple blue cornflowers. Delia exercised her creative whimsical side by choosing flowers representing both common and regal flowers. Her own bouquet was fashioned from white daisies and white roses. The music she chose to begin the ceremony was a fusion of contemporary and classical. The Bridesmaids entered to the Beatle's, "Here Comes the Sun" and then the organ shifted dramatically to Wagner's Bridal Chorus, "Here Comes the Bride."

Delia dazzled James when she appeared in layers and layers of white silk at the country church door. He felt the power of the symbolism for a moment and thought deeper than words: "My bride is crossing the threshold of a church door carrying a mirror of our child within... Our marriage *is* a marriage made in heaven. Her beautiful wedding gown was cut low at the back; the soft silk fell like chiffon clouds to create a dramatic train trailing behind. Delia's mother who was too unwell to make the trip had embroidered the train with island birds and flowers. Delia proudly wore James' grandmother's diamond tiara to fasten her bridal veil to the elegant Victorian style upsweep of her hair. A few wisps fell softly on each side of her coffee colored skin and brown almond eyes. She wore the simple diamond earrings James mother wore in her own wedding to James' father, so many years ago.

Delia began to tremble when she saw James. He looked handsome in his black tuxedo and when she looked at him standing next to her, and she saw his face thrilled with love and desire for her. Her heart was so full. She thought it might burst when they slid their wedding rings on each other's fingers. They were the perfect sign of their love.

CHAPTER *58*

THE NEXT THREE DAYS WAS SPENT PACKING THEIR BAGS TO GO TO SOUTH of France where James and Delia were going to spend their Honeymoon. Delia was very excited to have time with James as the new Mrs. Hicks. They flew from London to Niece which is right on the border of Italy. James brought her here because Delia loved to see all styles of art, and Niece was known to have some of the most beautiful art museums in the world. He booked their hotel reservation at the Sheraton hotel in Niece for two days and then he planned to fly his bride down to St. Tropez and stay in the same private beach villa where they conceived their son on New Year's Eve.

They both agreed that the French Riviera was one of the most beautiful places in the world. They enjoyed dining in the finest French cafes that bordered the beach. The weather was warm and they wanted to drink in the sunshine and sea air before returning to England. Delia was now in her sixth month of pregnancy and needed bed rest every afternoon. She didn't feel like indulging in the glamorous lifestyle, but she was happier than she had ever been in her life. All she needed was James by her side and the kicking of her baby inside to make her happy. She and James enjoyed simple pleasures together while they lounged in Saint Tropez. Even just walking on the beach at sunset, when the sky and the water turned coral and blue, or discovering an unbroken seashell on the beach, made their hearts happy. They had given up the party scene and especially drinking alcohol during Delia's pregnancy. All their conversations and activities centered on what was best for the baby. Delia liked this simple lifestyle and she loved James even more for being such a faithful caring husband and father to be.

CHAPTER *59*

THE BABY WAS DUE OCTOBER 1ST, BUT DELIA'S WATER BROKE IN THE middle of the night on September 29th. Her labor was quick and intense and on Michaela's, James Michael Hicks entered the world at 3 AM. James Senior was so happy to be a father that for the first time in his life he felt like his feet didn't touch the ground. For three days, he floated around Parliament carrying the footprint of his son in his pocket and handing out cigars. Delia miraculously recovered quickly.

When she called Victoria to share the good news, she found out from Chris that Victoria still had not delivered her baby and was headed to the hospital for a Caesarian. Delia called her in the hospital and joked with her "that at last Delia's large hips helped her to do something better than Victoria." They both laughed and Victoria was wheeled into the delivery room for surgery. Victoria's healthy little boy came flying out of her womb on October 14th, at 10 AM, two weeks late. They named him Christopher Junior after his father Chris and also because he was born on Christopher Columbus Day. When Victoria called from her hospital bed, she told Delia that her son liked floating in the water too long and weighed in at 9lbs and 6 ounces!"

"Wow, Vic, he likes eating almost as much as you!" They both laughed and made plans to visit when their babies were old enough to fly.

"Yes, long distance relationships are difficult", Victoria quipped of Delia's and James's wedding and the crown miracle son, "especially when you have children!"

Victoria ended by saying that Chris had asked her to marry him after witnessing the beauty of their wedding and the miracle birth of their son.

"Oh, Victoria! Congratulations! Most of what Maria the fortuneteller predicted has come true!"

And the best friends said goodbye but reminded each other that their goodbyes were not forever.

CHAPTER 60

$\mathcal{N}$ OVEMBER PASSED QUICKLY FOR DELIA IN A BLUR OF DIAPERS AND bottles and sleepless nights tending to the baby. James returned home every weekend to Manor Heights and was inseparable from his wife and new baby son.

James would tell her religiously every day: "Delia, you have made me the happiest politician in the world. I love you forever. And I am forever grateful for my son. I truly feel without James Junior and your love, I would have no future. I am looking forward to the Christmas break when I can relax in your arms and be at home full time. There is so much stress and conflict on the Parliament floor these days."

James's parents exuded pride and joy to finally be grandparents. His mother, Joanna, took a sabbatical from teaching, and moved into the guest room to help Delia with the baby during the week when James was away at Parliament

Joanna said to her daughter-in-law every night like a song of Thanksgiving: "Thank you Delia for making James a proud father and for allowing me to be a doting grandmother to my only grandson."

They made plans for celebrating Advent and Christmas at Manor Heights this year. Joanna offered to organize the cleaning, the cooking, the shopping, and the decorations. She had already made a shopping list of toys for her grandson's first Christmas.

Delia was especially thankful for the love of her new family. They made every fear she ever had of being rejected as an outsider seem ludicrous.

CHAPTER 61

ECEMBER ARRIVED WITH GRAY SKIES AND TRAGIC NEWS. DELIA WOULD now understand the mystery of Maria's fortuneteller predictions that she would marry a prosperous man who would bring her luck, but that the marriage wouldn't last. This Christmas would be the opposite of last year. Her joy was turned to mourning. Fiona called to break the news to her. In a heartbroken voice, she shared that he was gone.

"What do you mean 'gone', Fiona? Gone forever? NO! This can't be true! Oh, my God, Fiona! How? When? Where?" She cried passionately... as if these questions even mattered now.

"He was in his seat in parliament, when they say he suddenly slumped over...profusely sweating...they loosened his tie and stretched him out on the floor...but it was of no use...he was gone...a massive heart attack they said." Fiona began to sob.

"Do you mean James is *dead*, Fiona?" Delia asked now in a cold voice so often used by those who are numb with shock.

"Yes, Delia," Fiona said still sobbing, "my brother, your husband... your baby's father is dead."

Delia did not attend the pomp and circumstance surrounding his funeral. She had collapsed at the news and was too weak to attend. She made plans to take James Jr. home to the islands to meet his other grandparents. She needed to escape the scrutiny of the public eye. She needed the comforts of home...the healing balm of Savu Island breezes and the warm enveloping sunshine. Auntie Fiona would accompany Delia back to the island of her birth and tend to the needs of her tiny helpless baby for several months until Delia was healed.

Before returning to the islands to visit her parents, Delia road to the rocky cliffs overlooking the North Sea. A lone sea gull fought the winds blowing in from the turbulent salty water. She held her baby, bundled and warm, close to her heart. As she watched the storm clouds building, they seemed to form a massive open door. The sun broke through the cloud door. One ray touched the top of her baby's head as if giving a father's blessing-a heavenly benediction. She remembered that James had once said when they had discovered her pregnancy that some marriages are made in Heaven...

At that moment, James Junior glanced up at his mother, with his clear blue eyes, and for a moment Delia felt she was looking into the mirror of his father. "Is love a door or a mirror or both?" she wondered. She glanced back towards the sea and knew the silent answer: Love is forever.

Printed in the United States
By Bookmasters